The Proposal

Even the book morphs!
Flip the pages
and check it out!

titles in Large-Print Editions:

The Proposal

K.A. Applegate

Gareth Stevens Publishing
A WORLD ALMANAC EDUCATION GROUP COMPANY

The author wishes to thank Jeffrey Zuehlke for
his help in preparing this manuscript.

For Wayne and Kathy

And for Michael and Jake

**For a free color catalog describing Gareth Stevens' list
of high-quality books and multimedia programs, call
1-800-542-2595 (USA) or 1-800-461-9120 (Canada).
Gareth Stevens Publishing's Fax: (414) 332-3567.**

Library of Congress Cataloging-in-Publication Data available upon request
from publisher. Fax: (414) 332-3567 for the attention of the Publishing
Records Department.

ISBN 0-8368-2758-9

This edition first published in 2000 by
Gareth Stevens Publishing
A World Almanac Education Group Company
330 West Olive Street, Suite 100
Milwaukee, WI 53212 USA

Published by Gareth Stevens, Inc., 330 West Olive Street,
Suite 100, Milwaukee, Wisconsin 53212 in large print by
arrangement with Scholastic Inc., 555 Broadway, New York,
New York 10012.

1 2 3 4 5 6 7 8 9 04 03 02 01 00

CHAPTER 1

My name is Marco.

But you can call me "Marco the Mighty." Or "Most Exalted Destroyer of My Pride." You can cower before my mighty thumbs and beg for mercy, but you'll be crushed just the same.

For I am the lord of the PlayStation.

Pick a game. Any game. Tekken. Duke Nukem. NFL Blitz. Whatever. Practice all you want. I'll still beat you. I'll crush you like Doc Martens crush ants. I'll —

"The phone's ringing," my dad said, setting down his controller.

"You can't stop now," I cried. "I was gonna score on this next play!"

"It's fifty-six to nothing," he muttered. "I'll forfeit this one."

"But —"

But he'd already picked up the phone.

"Hello? Oh, hi! How are you?" His voice was so sweet and sticky you could have poured it over pancakes.

"Oh, brother," I mumbled.

"I'm doing great," he continued, a big dopey smile on his face. "Marco and I were just playing video games. Uh-huh. Sure." He looked at me. "Nora says hi."

I nodded. I grabbed the remote control. Switched the TV back to cable mode and turned the volume up loud enough to drown out his voice.

My dad has a girlfriend. And I think it's serious. I'm used to this quiet, low-key, unexpressive guy. But ever since he started dating this woman, he's been Mr. Personality. Smiling for no reason. Singing in the shower. Laughing at all my lame jokes like I was Chris Rock. He's even developed this annoying habit of hugging me for no good reason.

I mean, I'm happy for him. Really. When my mom disappeared over two years ago, my dad lost it. For a long time, he was little more than a zombie. Sometimes I thought he'd never recover.

A few months back he pulled himself out of

it. Things went back to normal. Or as normal as my life could be — until he met this woman.

Your dad being in love with someone who isn't your mother is a pretty normal problem, I guess. I mean, he's old, but he's not exactly using a walker and getting seniors' discounts at the Steak and Ale. Maybe you've dealt with the same thing yourself. Maybe you're dealing with it right now. Maybe this problem makes you feel like the weight of the world is on your shoulders.

Yeah, well, boo hoo. Sorry, kids. But you have no idea about the weight of the world. 'Cause it's on *my* shoulders.

See, not only do I live with a lovesick father. I'm also trying to save the world from being enslaved by evil, parasitic aliens.

To which you respond, "Ooooookay, dude forgot his medication."

I'm not crazy. And not lying. I'm telling the truth.

They're called Yeerks. They're from another galaxy. Gray, sluglike creatures that slide into your ear, flatten out inside your brain, and take control of your mind and body. Forcing you to do anything they want. Anything.

Right now, their invasion is a secret. Very few people know about it. Most of the people who do are their slaves. We call them Controllers. I don't know how many people the Yeerks have turned into Controllers. I don't think I want to know.

There are a handful of us fighting the Yeerks. A handful. As in four kids, an alien, and a red-tailed hawk.

Come to think of it, maybe I did forget my meds.

We call ourselves Animorphs. We have the ability to turn into any animal we touch. It may not sound like much of a weapon, but you'd be surprised. We've done plenty to hurt the Yeerks, and we're not through yet.

The Yeerks would love to get us. They'd love to make me and my friends their slaves so they could use our morphing powers to conquer the rest of the world.

That's why I don't tell you my last name. And that's why I won't tell you where I live. City or state. I want to stay anonymous. Anonymous equals alive. Maybe.

"Well, I really had a great time, too," my dad gushed into the phone.

As if the Yeerks aren't enough for me to deal with — this woman my dad has gone all Sweet'n Low for? She just happens to be a teacher at my school. My math teacher. Ms. Robbinette.

It's enough to make you want to ban parent/teacher conferences.

I turned the TV up a little more, hoping my

dad would get the hint and leave the room. He didn't.

There was nothing on TV worth watching. Lousy game shows. Corny old movies. Boring murder mysteries. Prime-time soap operas. But I continued to flip channels like a robot stuck on the same mindless function.

I stopped on a talk show I'd seen a few times before. *Contact Point.* It was hosted by some guy with a three-word name. William Roger Tennant.

Not your typical talk show. No audience. No guests. No comedy monologue. Just this Tennant guy, sitting cross-legged in a big comfy chair, surrounded by six-foot-tall Lava lamps, a bottle of designer water at his side.

People called in with problems, and he gave them helpful advice. There was something about the guy that made you want to like him. He was so relaxed. Like nothing could possibly bother him. And he seemed to be actually interested in what people had to say. Every caller was the most fascinating person he'd ever spoken to.

I don't know why I kept watching. I'm not a talk show kind of person. Maybe it was because I was hoping William Roger Tennant would say something to make me feel better. See, there's another complication to my dad's having a girl-friend. A serious one.

But William Roger Tennant didn't say anything that made me feel better. He said something that made me even sicker than my dad's middle-aged Romeo impersonation.

A woman caller was complaining about being lonely. She was retired. Many of her friends had passed away in recent years. She was having a hard time meeting people.

William Roger Tennant listened intently to her complaint. Looked thoughtfully at the camera.

"Marie," he said, "I know a great place where you can make friends. It's called The Sharing."

CHAPTER 2

"The Sharing?" I said, feeling a chill run up my spine.

"The Sharing?" the woman replied.

"Yes, The Sharing." William Roger Tennant leaned forward in his chair. Smiled hypnotically at the camera. "It's a wonderful organization," he said. "The Sharing is all about meeting people. Having fun together. Making the world a better place. It's changed so many people's lives for the better. I'm sure it could help you."

I stared hard at the screen.

The Sharing. Yeah, it was a place for people to get together and have fun. Go to barbecues. Sing songs. But William Roger Tennant had left out a key detail.

7

The Sharing is a front organization for the Yeerks. They use it to recruit humans. They get people to join, earn their trust, then turn them into Controllers.

My best friend Jake, the leader of our group? His brother Tom joined The Sharing a while ago. He's a Controller now. Mr. Chapman, our assistant principal, is also a member and a Controller. And you thought *your* assistant principal was evil.

And now this William Roger Tennant guy was on TV, recruiting innocent people for slavery.

William Roger Tennant. A smiling, bearded face. Light brown hair pulled back into a ponytail. Faded jeans and a casual button-down shirt. Everything about him was laid-back. Easygoing. Cool.

But behind it all, behind those warm, smiling blue eyes, was an evil alien slug, bent on making every single human being on the face of the earth a helpless slave.

That's the scariest thing of all about the Yeerks. You can't tell just by looking who's a Controller and who's not.

"Why don't you tell me where you live, Marie?" William Roger Tennant said to the caller. "I'll give you the number of a Sharing group near you."

I had to call Jake. Didn't want to, but had to. Didn't I?

Let it go, Marco, I told myself. *You know how this ends up: all of us screaming and running and maybe this time not making it out alive. Let it go.*

My dad hung up the phone, that goofy smile still stuck on his face. He sat down on the couch next to me and picked up his PlayStation gamepad.

"So, you ready to humiliate me some more?" he said.

I sighed. "I have to call Jake."

"Why?"

"Good question."

I used the phone in the kitchen to set up a meeting with the rest of the gang. In the carefully nonspecific way we set up meetings.

Now I had to think up an excuse to leave the house. It was eight o'clock on a school night. My dad had specifically set aside some time to hang out with me. I didn't want to hurt his feelings.

"So what do you want to do now?" he asked when I walked back into the living room. "You need help with your homework? Maybe we could watch a movie or something?"

"Uh, well," I said, "I have to go over to Jake's house. I left something there."

His smile faded. "Oh. Well, couldn't he just give it to you at school tomorrow? It's eight o'clock already."

"I need it tonight." I prayed he wouldn't ask what was so important. When you lie, it's always a good idea to have the details figured out beforehand.

"Well, okay," he replied, frowning.

"I'll be back in a little while," I mumbled.

I was about to walk out the door when he called to me. "Say, Marco?"

"Yeah?" I looked back at him, sitting on the couch, a very sad look on his face. It was a look I hadn't seen in a long time. It was the same look he'd worn for two whole years after my mom disappeared.

"Are you mad at me?"

I shrugged. "No, Dad. Why would I be mad at you?"

"I know you still think about your mom a lot," he began. "I just want you to know I do, too."

"I know," I said.

"It's just that it's been a long time," my dad continued. "I can't grieve forever. I — we — need to move on. I hope you can understand that. I mean, Nora's a nice person, isn't she?"

Maybe if I was a better son, I could have said something to cheer him up. But I'm not and I couldn't.

"Yeah. She's okay," I said. "It's just weird, that's all."

I shut the door behind me and tried to control the guilt.

Yeah, I wanted my dad to be happy. But there was a really big problem with the whole Nora situation.

My mom may not really be dead.

CHAPTER 3

I took off my jeans, sweater, and shoes and stuffed them in a little cubbyhole I'd made in the corner of my garage. We never have figured out how to morph clothing, other than skin-tight stuff. Besides, a big bird of prey would look kind of conspicuous flying around in a pair of Levi's.

I tried to relax and focus on my morph. It was tough. I'd made my dad feel bad. I didn't like that. It wasn't his fault, any of it. How was he supposed to know his wife wasn't really dead?

Or at least, not for sure.

My mom, her body anyway, was Visser One. The original leader of the Yeerk invasion of Earth. My mom was a Controller.

She'd faked her own death when her assignment on Earth was up. She didn't want to leave any open questions as to what happened to my mother. So there was a boating accident. And for two years my dad and I thought she was gone.

Then I learned the truth. No way I could tell my dad. And the truth was, she was as good as dead. Probably.

I'd seen her last on a blasted mountaintop. I'd led her there, me, her son, as part of a plan to take down Vissers One and Three.

The last I'd seen her she went off a cliff. No body had turned up, but that may have just been the Yeerks cleaning up their own mess.

For two years, dead. Then alive. And now?

It was a totally impossible situation.

I was almost glad to have this mission. As dangerous as it was bound to be. It would keep my mind off Dad and Nora and all the hopeless conflicts I was feeling over it.

I concentrated on the animal I wanted to morph. Osprey. Fish-eating bird of prey. Eyes like lasers. Six-foot wingspan.

And I felt the changes begin.

Morphing is totally bizarre. It makes even the wildest and creepiest movie effects seem ordinary. There's something about watching your entire body completely change its shape that never ceases to freak you out.

ZWOOOOP!

13

I was shrinking. Rapidly. From five feet to four. To three. To two. The garbage cans my dad had bought at Home Depot were as big as three-story buildings now. The push broom leaning against the wall was as tall as a tree.

My bare feet quivered. My toes began to merge, to melt together, the way cookies melt into each other in the oven when you put them too close together on the pan.

Five stubby toes became three long slender ones. A fourth toe sprouted out of each of my ankles. Then a long, sharp talon slithered out of each toe.

Next, my skin started to itch.

Pfft! Pfft! Pfft!

The hairs on my arms started growing like superfast-growing grass. Then each long hair blossomed into a feather. Black feathers along my back. White feathers on my front.

Now my arms would transform themselves into wings. I would be able to fly. And as soon as the morph was complete, I could lose myself in the simple, straightforward mind of the osprey. At least for the time it took to fly to Cassie's.

Come on, come on, I urged myself. Osprey.

My eyes were supposed to go telescopic. Allowing me to spot glittering fish through reflective water.

They didn't. Instead, they began to grow

14

darker. Blurrier. Until I could see only dim shapes around me. A hazy combination of black, white, and gray.

My arms! They weren't becoming wings! What was happening? I felt them stretching out in front of me. The skin on my hands turning brittle, like armor. Fingers merging, becoming two barbed claws.

Something was wrong!

My face . . .

A pinprick on each cheek! Two long whisker-like hairs sprouted outward. Instinctively, I swept them in front of me, gauging the wind, the temperature, sensing my surroundings.

Antennae? Birds don't have antennae!

Dim eyes. Pincers. Antennae.

Lobster?

I was half-osprey, half-lobster?

A useless combination of mismatched parts.

I struggled to stand on the osprey's narrow legs. Dragged the lobster's heavy claws along the dirty garage floor. My antennae swept back and forth, faster and faster, desperately searching. For what?

Suddenly, the lobster's mind took over.

Panic! Fear!

Water! Where was the water!

I had lobster lungs and gills. But I was nowhere near water.

15

No. NO! This couldn't be happening.

The lobster's panic was intense. Desperately I tried to fight it.

Come on, Marco. Settle down. Just morph out and everything will be fine.

Morph out!

CHAPTER 4

It took half an hour to ride my bike to Cassie's parents' barn, aka the Wildlife Rehabilitation Clinic. A place where Cassie and her dad nurse sick and injured animals back to health.

Its walls are lined with cages. Pens and stalls house the larger guests. At any given time the barn is filled with all sorts of animals, from bald eagles to beavers to llamas. And like any barn, it's short on comfort and quiet, long on the aroma of sweet hay and animal feces.

But it is private.

I was still shaking when I went inside.

"It's about time you got here," Rachel growled. "I'm missing *Felicity.*"

Rachel is tall, blond, and beautiful. At first

glance, she seems like a perfectly typical self-centered, spoiled teenage girl.

Here's some advice, kids: Don't judge a book by its cover. If the Animorphs were a hockey team, Rachel would be our goon. She's always the first one to start a fight. Always the last one to surrender.

<You mean *we're* missing *Felicity*,> Tobias added from his perch in the rafters. Tobias is what the Andalites call a *nothlit*. He stayed in his red-tailed hawk morph for longer than two hours. Stay in a morph for longer than two hours, and it's not a morph anymore. It's yours to keep.

Now red-tailed hawk is his normal form. Although thanks to the Ellimist, he can morph like the rest of us.

"Isn't that romantic?" I said mockingly. "Blondie and Bird-boy watching TV together. So Rachel munches popcorn and Tobias eats road-kill? Romance! Must be something in the air."

"What's your problem, Marco, not enough fiber?" Rachel snapped.

Cassie shot me a look of disapproval that made me wince.

Okay, maybe I'd been a little harsh. I'd make it up to Tobias later.

"We were getting a little worried," Jake added with a tad more diplomacy. "We were about to fly out to your house to see if something was wrong."

Jake's the leader of our group. He's also been my best friend for as long as I can remember, despite the fact that we're very different people. Jake's the responsible, serious, leader-type. I'm the devil-may-care comedian.

At least that's what I often find it useful for people to think.

I shrugged. "I decided to ride my bike."

"You *what*?" Cassie said.

Cassie and Rachel are best friends. Like me and Jake, they're almost complete opposites. While Rachel's well dressed and prone to violence, Cassie's a slob and good and caring and strong — and usually right.

"I rode my bike," I repeated impatiently. "Weren't you the one giving me grief about never exercising? So I exercised."

No way was I going to tell the others about my morph freakout. That I'd barely managed to demorph before suffocating. That I had been too freaked to try morphing again.

A fluke, that's all it was. I'd been distracted, preoccupied. I must have lost focus. I was just going to put it out of my mind. Just forget that something that was already terrifying had gone to total nightmare.

<Ah, yes. Physical fitness,> Ax said in thought-speak. <But surely a special array of artificial skins is necessary. From "These Messages" on television, I have learned that fitness requires particular shoes and particular clothing. It is not possible to become physically fit dressed as you are, Marco.>

Ax, also known as Aximilli-Esgarrouth-Isthill, is our resident alien.

He's an Andalite. Think deer. Except with blue fur. And a humanoid torso growing out of the front of his body. A torso with skinny arms and seven-fingered hands.

Weird enough for you yet? But wait! There's more!

Andalites have human-shaped heads. With deerlike ears. No mouth. Eyes inside their skull, just like you and me. But on top of their heads they have an auxiliary pair attached to stalks that can twist and turn 360 degrees. Making it virtually impossible to sneak up behind them.

Ax also has a long tail with a blade on the end that could lop your head off before you even saw it twitch.

The Andalites invented morphing technology. It was Ax's brother Elfangor who gave us our powers. Shortly before he was murdered by Visser Three.

At this moment Ax was in his human morph, a

strangely attractive DNA combination of me, Jake, Rachel, and Cassie.

"*Anyway*," Rachel interrupted. "Was that the only reason we called this meeting? So Marco could work off some of his leftover baby fat?"

"I hope not," Jake said tightly. "I've got tons of homework."

"Anyone ever hear of a guy named William Roger Tennant?" I asked.

"Sure," Rachel answered. "The hippie guy. The one with that weird touchy-feely talk show with the Lava lamps. *Contact Point.*"

"Didn't he write all those *Men Are from Jupiter, Women Are from Venus* books?" Jake asked.

<I do not believe either Jupiter or Venus are inhabitable, certainly not by humans,> Ax said.

"Mars, not Jupiter," Cassie corrected.

<Mars may be marginally habitable.>

"Actually, some guys are from Uranus," Rachel said. Then she made a face. "Did I just say that? I'm spending too much time around you, Marco."

"I'm rubbing off on you."

"Different guy anyway," Rachel said. "But Tennant has written a lot of self-help books. My mom reads them. Reads 'em and for, like, two days she's all mellow, then it wears off."

<Self-help books?> Ax asked. <Are they similar to instruction manuals?>

21

<Not exactly, Ax-man,> Tobias said. <Self-help books are like instruction books for living.>

<Indeed? Instructions for living? Such as "Consume necessary nutrients"? "Breathe sufficient air"?>

"Hey! Ax just made a joke."

<I did?>

"Self-help as in wise advice," Cassie explained. *"Chicken Soup for Whatever. I'm Okay, You're Messed Up.* You know. They give you advice on how to live your life."

<Ah, yes. Like Oprah,> Ax replied. <She, too, enjoys chicken soup. But it must be low-fat and heart healthy.>

Ax has been a bit unusual — if that's possible — since he got a TV in his little woodsy hideout.

"Okay. Now, if we can slowly back out of the lunatic asylum and rejoin reality," Jake said impatiently. "Marco? You were saying?"

"I was just watching his show —"

Rachel cut me off. "You were watching William Roger Tennant? Marco looking for advice? On what? Coping with shortness?"

"I was just channel surfing," I yelled. "That's not the point! He's a Yeerk! He's using the show to recruit people for The Sharing."

<Uh-oh,> Tobias said.

"What exactly did Tennant say?" Jake asked.

I repeated Tennant's pitch to the elderly caller named Marie.

"We have to stop him," Cassie said simply.

"How?" Rachel asked, only half-joking. "Trash the studio?"

Like I said. If we were a hockey team —

"We could launch a direct attack," Jake said thoughtfully. "But what's to stop the Yeerks from moving Tennant to another studio? He'd be back on the air in a few days."

<The real problem is William Roger Tennant himself,> Tobias said. <We've got to find a way to get him off the air. Permanently.>

"Yeah, but how?" I said.

"We dig up some dirt on him," Rachel said. "Major smear campaign. That's how you take down a celebrity. Unless he's like a politician. Or an athlete. They're immune."

Jake frowned. "This means surveillance. We watch him, starting now. When we have the info we need, we take him down. Marco? Take Ax and see what you can find online. An address would be a good start."

"You know, I can surf the Web without Ax holding my hand."

"Yeah, but he can do it without wasting three hours cruising *Baywatch* Web sites."

"Oooh. Through the heart," I said, miming a knife in the chest.

"Then, given the time of day, Ax and Tobias? You take the first shifts. Marco and I will relieve you after school tomorrow. Probably bird morphs, as usual. Okay, Marco?"

I swallowed hard. Morphing. No big deal. Unless . . .

"Okay, Jake. No problemo."

CHAPTER 5

<This bites,> I said. <Why did we get stuck with the Saturday morning shift? I should be asleep right now. Or watching *The Powerpuff Girls*.>

Cassie and I were in seagull morph, on the top of the compound's east wall. A gust of wind came in from the ocean, forcing me to flap my wings to keep from falling off.

It had been three days since we'd started our surveillance of William Roger Tennant. Three days of watching and waiting.

And during those three days I'd had to morph several times. Not once did I have a problem. No mutant morphs. A huge relief.

But the fear still lingered. Why had it happened? Would it happen again? And if so, when?

It had turned out that William Roger Tennant owned a huge beachfront mansion. Three stories. Lots of windows. A compound filled with a variety of trees and shrubs. Hedges sculpted into animal shapes. A stone wall covered with ivy surrounded the property.

<You know why you're here,> Cassie replied. <You switched with Jake so you could watch the *South Park* marathon last night.>

<Yeah, but that was before I knew about *The Powerpuff Girls* marathon,> I grumbled. <They shouldn't have more than one marathon in a week. It's just wrong. And why are we still doing this stakeout, anyway? We know Tennant's a Controller. Ax and Tobias saw him sneak into the Yeerk pool through The Gap entrance yesterday morning. What we need is to get inside the house,> I added. <We've got a plan. Albeit a suicidal one. Why not just get it over with?>

<You know why,> Cassie said. <Rachel's on little sister duty this afternoon. We're going in tomorrow. Meanwhile, we're learning Tennant's habits.>

<But we know his habits! And in the past three days he hasn't done anything even remotely illegal or scandalous. The guy's a saint.>

<Yeah, I know,> Cassie agreed. <The guy's

26

squeaky clean. He's spent his entire life helping people. He's given millions to charity: Doctors Without Borders, the Humane Society, all kinds of diseases, the American Society for the Prevention of Cruelty to Animals. I mean, if I didn't know better, I'd love this guy. And he's got tons of famous friends —>

<Which is probably why the Yeerks wanted him on board,> I said. <He's a perfect recruiter.>

William Roger Tennant emerged from the compound, dressed in a dark blue running outfit. Did some stretches. Then started his jog along the beach.

<Like clockwork,> Cassie said.

<Let's go.> My spindly seagull legs pushed off the wall. I opened my wings to catch the warm breeze that was blowing off the water.

Every morning William Roger Tennant went for a forty-five-minute jog along the beach. Same path. Same speed. Same distance.

<Maybe he's not really a Controller after all,> I said. <Maybe he's an android. I mean, what kind of human keeps such a strict schedule?>

We kept Tennant's bouncing brown ponytail in our sights as he jogged along at his deliberate pace.

<Uh-huh,> Cassie agreed. <It's the same thing every day. From eight A.M. to eight-forty-five A.M. he goes jogging. Comes home, takes a

27

shower. Sits at his desk and works for a few hours. Writes on the computer. Makes a few phone calls. Eats lunch, at his desk. Feeds the birds. Talks to them. Then at five o'clock he hops in his limo and is driven to the TV studio.>

<You know, I kind of wish Tennant weren't a Controller. I mean, apart from the Yeerk in his head he's such a swell guy. I watch *Contact Point* and I want to tell him about my own problems.>

<Something bothering you, Marco?> Cassie asked.

<No, absolutely not.>

<Uh-huh. So it doesn't bother you that your dad is dating?>

<What? No way. My dad is seriously gaga over Ms. Robbinette. So what? Not my problem, his problem.>

I'd told the others about my dad dating my math teacher. Back in the beginning. I'd had to tell them that much. We had to make sure Ms. Robbinette wasn't a Controller. For three days we'd followed her. She'd never gone near any known Yeerk pool entrances.

<She seems nice,> Cassie said. <Aren't you happy for your dad?>

<Sure. Why not?> I said.

<Still, you're in a tough position,> Cassie said.

<Actually, I'm sorry I brought it up. I don't

28

want to talk about it. It's boring. I mean, who cares, right?>

<Okay.>

<I mean, the situation's bad enough,> I continued. So maybe I did want to talk about it. Just a little bit. <But does she have to be one of my teachers? Let alone my math teacher? And then there's Euclid.>

<Her toy poodle.>

<Satan with a perm. Simple commands like "sit," "stay," "heel" all mean the same thing to this dog: Bark at Marco. Jump on Marco. Bite Marco's ankle.>

For forty-five minutes we followed William Roger Tennant up the beach and then back to the compound. For forty-five minutes I vented. Cassie may or may not have listened. Every once in a while, she said <"uh-huh"> or <"bummer.">

By the time Tennant walked back through the gate of the compound, I felt a little better.

I had not mentioned the mutant morph.

<I know it's hard, but try to see the positive side of the situation,> Cassie said as we watched Tennant do his postjog stretches. <Your dad is happy. That's a good thing. Start there and maybe things will be okay.>

<Yeah,> I replied.

We landed on the stone wall encircling the compound. Watched William Roger Tennant

29

cross the courtyard and go inside through the main entrance.

From our perch we could see into Tennant's office. It was hard not to. Two of the walls were made almost entirely of glass. The room had an amazing ocean view.

<I mean, it probably doesn't matter anyway. Our chances of surviving tomorrow's mission are slim to none.>

The office door opened. William Roger Tennant, now dressed in his usual faded jeans and rumpled button-down oxford shirt, walked over to his desk and sat down. He raised his left hand close to his face.

Perched on his finger was a gray feathered creature about a foot long. He raised it up to his lips and gave it a dainty little kiss.

William Roger Tennant had a large collection of domestic birds. Finches. Parakeets. And cockatiels.

The plan was for five of us to morph cockatiels and search his house.

Five tiny, helpless birds fluttering around inside the house of a powerful Yeerk.

We'd get caught, I'd get crushed, I wouldn't even have to think about my dad and the math teacher.

CHAPTER 6

Cockatiels.

According to one of Cassie's bird books, a species originally from Australia. About a foot long, from the crescent-shaped plume of feathers sprouting from the top of its head to the tip of its long gray-feathered tail.

Said to be highly intelligent. Even capable of mimicking human speech. We'd morphed parrots once, long ago. Just to mess with some people's heads. This would be different. We'd be going seriously in harm's way, which brought to mind the image of me yelling, "Squuuuaaawwk, don't kill me, squuaaawwk!"

William Roger Tennant owned ten cockatiels. Along with the other birds they seemed to have free reign of the house, although they spent most of their time in an open aviary. All of which made them perfect morphs for spying on Tennant.

Maybe too perfect.

<Remember. This could be a trap,> Jake said. <Tennant knows about the "Andalite bandits." He knows that at some point we'll try to come after him. What better way to kill us than by luring us into his house in vulnerable morphs?>

<What better way to *capture* us,> I replied, jerking my head left, right, left, back.

<That's why we're spreading out,> Jake said. <We get in and morph the cockatiels. Marco and Rachel, you stick with Tennant. Cassie, Ax and I will search the house. If one group runs into trouble, the other group hides and does battle morphs. Tobias will stay outside and let us know if the Yeerks send in reinforcements.>

He suddenly sat up on his haunches, looked back, left, focused, right, up.

As far as we knew, William Roger Tennant lived alone with his posse of birds. A housekeeping service came in and cleaned the mansion every morning. Had to be every day what with birds messing everywhere.

Except for Tennant and the birds, the house was empty all afternoon.

We hoped.

<We don't know what's in the basement, Jake,> I pointed out as I jerked my head left, left, right, up. <What if Tennant's got a dozen Hork-Bajir down there? You going to be able to get away in time to morph?>

<We call for you and Rachel. Do you have a problem with this plan, Marco?>

<No,> I replied quickly. What was I going to do? Tell everyone I suddenly wasn't sure they should be relying on me? That I wasn't sure I could morph in an emergency? Just as we were about to go into a very, very dangerous mission? No. <Of course not. Just want to be sure we know the risks.>

<If Jake's done explaining and Marco's done whining, maybe we can get down to business,> Rachel said. <This morph does not like to sit still.>

<Yes,> Ax added. <This is a very energetic creature.>

The four of us had acquired squirrel morphs. Cassie already had one. Our morphs were like the squirrels scampering around your backyard right now. Gray, brown, and white fur. Long, twitchy bushy tail. Big, twitchy dark brown eyes. More energy than a hyperactive kid after a dozen cups of coffee.

Between the five of us we were jerking our heads, looking in every possible direction, about nine times a second.

<Okay. Let's go,> Jake said. He raced up the telephone pole. I raced up after him. So cool! The squirrel might as well have been running horizontally. Tiny little claws instantly found tiny little handholds.

Then, onto a phone line that led to the house. I looked out along that long, swooping wire and felt the squirrel's utter confidence. Walk on a wire? Sure, why not?

Off we went, single file of course, zipping along without a care in the world aside from the incessant, jerky, twitchy caution. I felt rather than saw Tobias in the air above us. The squirrel was not happy about his shadow.

Along the wire. Off onto a nearby tree branch. Then down onto the top of a stone wall. Then down to the ground in the courtyard.

<We are the ultimate burglars,> Rachel said.

She jumped from the stone wall to a large oak and motored over the courtyard to Tennant's house.

<Ax?> Jake said, stopping to stare with squirrel intensity at the alarm junction.

<The creature's digits are quite nimble,> Ax said. <There should be no problem.>

The house was protected by a high-tech burglar alarm system. It took Ax about fifteen seconds to disarm it, working away with his little squirrel hands and chattering in squirrelese the whole time.

It was a bright, sunny day. Plenty of open windows. All had screens. But we'd come up with an insanely brilliant plan to get through the screens. A plan requiring very sophisticated human technology.

<Here goes,> Jake said. He hopped onto a narrow first-floor windowsill, a two-inch-long Swiss Army knife clenched in his teeth.

The window opened into a library a few doors down the hall from Tennant's office. Right next to the aviary. We'd seen Tennant use the library only once, at night.

Cassie had told us we probably didn't want to sneak directly into the aviary. Cockatiels can be kind of nervous. And they can be very loud when upset.

Jake jabbed the blade of the knife into the screen and pushed down on it, making an inch-long incision. Then he stuck his nose in the hole, bit on the screen, and ripped it open another inch.

<Okay, we're in.> Jake tossed the knife back down to the ground. <Tobias? Grab that for me. We don't want to leave any clues.>

Jake slipped through the hole. We followed,

one by one, until the five of us were inside. Except for a couple of reading chairs, a floor lamp, and a massive bookcase, the room was bare.

<Okay,> Jake said. <Marco and Rachel. You go first.>

<When we're all done acquiring we'll see if we can close off the aviary,> Cassie said. <We don't want Tennant seeing double.>

<Once Tennant sits down at his desk, he's usually there all afternoon,> Jake went on. <We'll just take a buzz around the place and leave without his ever knowing we were here.>

<Did you have to say that?> I groaned. <Now you've jinxed us.>

<Let's do it,> Rachel said, already beginning to demorph.

I did the same, although without quite as much enthusiasm.

It's one thing to be a squirrel in a strange home. You feel innocent, somehow. But to stand there as a normal kid wearing a stupid morphing outfit, that feels pretty criminal.

Our footsteps were heavy. Our movements were slow. We were way big to hide. And no one was going to overlook us. "Oh, some kids in the library? I didn't even notice."

We finished demorphing. I felt the need to put my finger to my lips to indicate to Rachel

that we had to be quiet. She felt the need to respond with a toxic "Duh!" look.

We slipped out of the library and into the
aviary next door.

It was a big, high-ceilinged room, maybe
three floors tall altogether. Glass-walled like a
greenhouse, which it was, partly, with several
large trees and plants everywhere. It was like an
exhibit at the zoo. The birdhouse.

The birds mostly sat in the trees. Some flew,
but most just hung out. They shifted on their
perches when Rachel and I entered. Especially
the cockatiels. As if on cue, the plume of feathers on the foreheads of all ten shot straight up in
the air.

"Twooooit! Twooooit! Twooooit! Twooooit!"

"Yow. That's loud," I said.

Rachel walked slowly up to one of the low
branches, her hands held high in a "you can trust
me" position. Like a cop trying to negotiate with
a gunman.

"Hi, birdie," she whispered. "Don't worry. I
won't hurt you."

"Twooit! Twooit!"

I targeted a bird that seemed to be chewing
its toes while it stood on one foot. As I got near
the bird decided it had eaten enough toe.

"Twooit! Twoooit! Twooooit!"

37

He shuffled back and forth on his perch. Bobbed his head frantically.

I stuck my hand toward him. "You're tame, right?" I whispered.

"Marco, watch out!" Rachel hissed.

Too late.

CHAPTER 7

"Owww!" I cried, jerking my hand back.

"Shhhhhh!!!" Rachel hissed.

"He took a chunk out of my finger," I whispered as I bounced around, holding my finger with my other hand.

"Didn't you listen to Cassie?" Rachel whispered back. "She said you have to approach the birds in a nonthreatening way."

"I didn't threaten him! But *now* I'm going to threaten him."

I glared at my beady-eyed opponent. He turned his head to one side and winked at me triumphantly. Once I touched him, it would be easy enough. The acquiring process puts the animal into a kind of trance.

It was the touching part that made me nervous. That plus the fact that I expected Tennant to show up looking wise and mellow and incinerate me with a wise, mellow Dracon beam.

Rachel had already acquired her bird and begun to morph.

<Hey, guys.> Tobias called from high above. <Tennant just went into his office. And, um, Marco? Some reason why you're dancing?>

"Very funny," I muttered.

I reached my hand back toward the bird. Slowly.

"That's how you're supposed to nyufgh —" Rachel whispered as her mouth shrank and hardened into a beak.

The cockatiel backed away and cocked his head to strike. I dived! Wrapped my hand around him. Hah! Swallowed the pain as he took another vicious peck at my hand.

"Go nighty-night, you monster."

He went into the trance.

Seconds later, I set him back on his perch. I resisted the impulse to yank out one or two feathers as payback. Took a deep breath and tried to focus.

Just relax, I told myself. *Let the morph happen. Be the bird.* But my heart was still pounding. And my finger still hurt.

The first thing to change was my head. It began to shrink. From normal size to the size of a cantaloupe. To grapefruit. To orange. To just slightly bigger than a cherry tomato.

<Oh, that's a nice look,> Rachel said. She'd finished her morph and was perched on top of a cage. <Now your head finally matches the size of your brain.>

I would have made a witty response, but my mouth was turning hard like a fingernail. Slowly growing out of my face and forming a sharp, hooked beak.

My skin felt ticklish, then began to ripple. Feathers. I looked at my hands. From each of my pointer fingers, one gray feather sprouted. Then a second. Then a third. More feathers sprouted. Faster and faster. A flood of feathers rolling down my arms like a swollen river raging through a valley. Until I was covered with them head to toe.

The trees and bushes seemed to shoot up into the air as I shrank. Down to a very vulnerable size. A foot long. Weighing only a few ounces.

Then my tiny human feet began to change. My five toes mushed together. Two long toes sprouted from the front of the mush. Two more sprouted out of where my ankle had been.

My legs shrank until they were barely an inch long. Just short stumps growing out of my baseball-sized body. My shoulders slid down my back. My miniature arms stretched outward like branches on a tree, flattening themselves into lushly feathered gray wings.

Suddenly, the bird's incredible sense of hearing kicked in. I could hear every flutter of every feather of every bird in the room. One was grinding his beak. Another was digging through his food, looking for a particular seed. And every cockatiel was talking, laughing, singing!

"Twoooit, twoooit, twoooit," I said excitedly.

<Marco, what are you doing?> Rachel said.

"Twoooit, twoooit, twoooit!" <I'm singing,> I said. "Twoooit! Twoooit!"

The morph had gone okay. Here I was, on a mission. A dangerous mission. And no mixed-morph. I'd done it! Maybe the osprey/lobster fiasco was just a freak occurrence.

I fluttered around the room. <This morph rocks!>

"Twooi-twooi-twooit!"

<Marco? Rachel?> Jake. Calling from the library.

<Uh, yeah?>

<Is everything all right in there?>

<Yeah,> Rachel said tightly. <Why wouldn't it be?>

<Well, it's been almost ten minutes since you guys went in there . . .>

<No way. Ten minutes?> I laughed.

<Guys, remember the mission? William Roger Tennant?>

<Yeah, Jake. No problem.> To me Rachel said, <Get a grip, Marco. Or I'm telling Jake to pull you off this mission right now.>

My own mind began to get the upper hand on the cockatiel's. My own personality pushed through. The bird's joy faded, replaced by another emotion.

Fear.

Not an improvement.

CHAPTER 8

We fluttered out of the aviary. Turned left toward Tennant's office.

The paranoid instincts of the prey animal began to grow. These birds were all tame, but tameness didn't change DNA. Down deep in its DNA this bird was still afraid. It didn't want to be indoors. It didn't like not being able to see in all directions. You never knew when a snake might slither up.

Zoom! We flew through a doorway. Zoom! Around some tall potted plants. Zoom! Down a hallway with very little clearance on either side.

The bird had excellent vision. Plenty good enough to keep track of where we were going. And after three days on surveillance I felt like I knew Tennant's house.

Zoom! Around a corner, and we were there. Just outside the office.

<Okay, here we go,> Rachel said and disappeared through the open door.

The room was huge. Two of the walls were glass, gigantic windows overlooking the ocean. The other two walls, including the one with the door, were lined with very large, very full bookshelves. In the middle of the room, a huge oak desk faced the ocean.

The desk itself was impeccably neat and organized. On it sat a laptop computer, a telephone, and a couple of T-shaped bird stands. William Roger Tennant was using the computer. He was so absorbed in his work, he didn't seem to notice our entrance.

<So far, so good.> Rachel flared her wings and landed on one of the bird stands. I landed on the other.

<What's he writing?> I asked. <I can't read the monitor from this perch.>

I shuffled along the horizontal pole, hoping to get a better viewing angle. And appear natural.

<Here, let me try.> Rachel hopped off her perch, fluttered through the air, and landed right on top of Tennant's head. He didn't even bat an eye.

<Ah, the subtle approach.>

<I've seen the other birds do it all the time,>

45

she said. <He's writing a letter. A thank-you letter.>

<Who to?>

<No address yet.>

Tennant maneuvered his mouse and double-clicked.

<He's doing a mail merge,> Rachel said. <Huh. It's a letter to the president of one of the TV networks.>

<Why would Tennant be writing to the head of a network? Didn't like last week's *ER*?>

Brrrrrrrrrring!

<Aaaaaaahh!!> I cried.

<Geez, that's loud!> Rachel said. <These birds have good hearing.>

Brrrrrrrrrring!

William Roger stared at the phone as if it were a diseased enemy.

Brrrrrrrrrring!

Finally, he picked up the receiver. His hand was shaking just a bit.

"Hello?"

I couldn't make out the voice on the other end. But I knew who it was. And my own fear seemed to infect the cockatiel's body. I could feel its feathers bristling with panic. Its little heart begin to beat like a machine gun's rapid firing.

"Yes, Visser," William Roger Tennant said

with all the enthusiasm people usually reserve for hearing a terminal diagnosis from their doctor.

<Visser Three,> Rachel hissed.

Visser Three. Our most feared and hated enemy. The leader of the Yeerk invasion of Earth. The only Yeerk to have infested an Andalite. The only Yeerk with the power to morph.

I stuck my beak beneath one of my wings and plucked out a few feathers. Dropped them on the desk. I stuck my beak under my other wing and plucked out a few more feathers.

"Everything is going just fine," Tennant muttered.

"Twooit!" I blurted out.

"I'm just finishing that letter now, Visser."

"Twooit! Twooit!"

<Marco? What are you doing?> Rachel hissed.

"Twooit! Twooit! Twooit!"

What was wrong with me? I was losing control of the morph! Couldn't keep it from chirping. From plucking out its own feathers. From rocking, back and forth. Back and forth.

"Yes, Visser. The construction of that Kandrona is coming along right on schedule."

"Twooit! Twooit! Twooit! Twooit!"

<Marco! Shut! Up!>

<I can't,> I cried. <I can't help it!>

Such a simple morph. An intelligent but tiny brain. And my human brain couldn't conquer it!

I plucked a few more feathers and dropped them on the desk. Tennant gave me a sharp glare.

"Twoooit! Twoooooit! Twoooooooit!"

"Yes, Visser. The president of the network will be at the Solid Citizen Awards banquet this weekend. As you know, I will be receiving an award. I fully expect the human to take the occasion to offer me a prime-time slot for the coming season."

<He's going to prime-time TV? Figures. It's not like UPN needs him or anything,> Rachel said.

"Twoooit! Twoooit! Twoooit!"

<Marco? How about, get a grip?>

"Twoooooit! Twoooooit! Twoooooooooit!"

"Excuse me, Visser." Tennant cupped his hand over the phone and looked at me. And then he screamed. "Shut up, you filthy creature!"

"Twirt," I sputtered lamely.

Tennant continued his phone conversation.

"No, Visser, I don't feel I should kill the bird. I must maintain William Roger Tennant's animal-loving image. But yes, these cockatiels are very annoying."

Pause.

Then, "Yes, Visser, the day will come when we

exterminate all irrelevant creatures. Looking forward to it."

Suddenly, I had an urge.

<Rachel? I think I'm going to . . . never mind.
I just did.>

It took hardly any effort. A completely natural
thing to do. If it hadn't been so easy, I might
have been able to control myself.

<Yeah, that was a good idea, Marco,> Rachel
said. <This guy's already popping veins in his
head and you mess on his desk.>

"Yes, Visser. Yes, Visser. Yes, Visser." Then,
"Oh, I *am* going to kill you," William Roger Tennant cried as he slammed down the receiver.

<Who? Who's he going to kill — me, or Visser Three?>

CHAPTER 9

The happiness guru picked up a remote control and punched a button. Shades began to lower across all the windows. He was making sure no one saw him.

Uh-oh.

"Why you —" William Roger Tennant growled.

<I think it's you, Marco! Bail!> Rachel yelled.

I spread my wings and pushed off the stand. Tennant dove across the desk, arm outstretched. He grabbed for me, but missed.

<Move! Move!> Rachel shouted as she flew

50

into the hallway. <Jake. Guys. We've got a problem!>

I shot toward the door.

"Not so fast, little birdie," Tennant hissed.

My super-keen ears heard it coming. A book.
A big, hardcover book.

BONK!

It nailed me. I fell to the carpet. Wind
knocked out of me. Stunned. Brain whirling. Im-
ages of big snakes coming down a branch for me.

Tennant pounced on me. Snatched me up in
his hands and pressed his thumbs into my chest.
Started to squeeze.

"I'll teach you to crap on my desk, you
little —"

My ribs! Bending! Collapsing!

My lungs! About to explode! Blood surging to
my head!

<Aaaaaaaaaaaaarrrrrrrgghhhhhhhhhh!> I was
screaming.

<Marco! Hang on! Hang on!>

My eyes were locked on Tennant's face. He
was gritting his teeth. His pale blue eyes bulged,
suddenly shot through with red veins. A vein in
his temple swelled and throbbed.

He looked like he was going to explode, erupt
like a broken cyst. But his hands were no longer
tightening.

51

Then I got it. The Yeerk was struggling. Battling something within the body. Battling William Roger Tennant. The *real* human named William Roger Tennant.

"Oh, little birdie, little birdie," Tennant whispered. "If only you could hear my host's cries of anguish. His pleas to spare your worthless life. Humans! Such a weak, sentimental species."

Then he loosened his grip and began to stroke my feathers.

"Oh, how I would love to kill you," he crooned. "If for no other reason than to hear the cries of agony from this pathetic host's tortured mind, oh yes, oh yes. But I won't kill you. Not now. No, no, no. I'm looking forward to the day when I can kill all of you horrible little creatures at once! Oh, what joy that will be! Perhaps such carnage will be enough to break this human's spirit, once and for all!"

Still, he kept stroking me. Eyes glittering. Sweat popping out in beads on his forehead.

I tried to relax. Tried to remain calm. He was going to let me go. Wasn't he? He didn't seem to notice that Rachel had returned. Was fluttering overhead, watching, ready to strike.

Like she could inflict serious harm in cockatiel morph.

<The others are coming, Marco,> she said. <Stay calm! They're doing battle morphs.>

"When I was first given this host," William Roger Tennant went on, his voice mellowing, almost as if he were speaking to an audience of rapt TV viewers, "I never thought my greatest challenge would be having to be as patient, as kind, as loving as this maundering, mewling, pathetic human. Who would have thought it would be so difficult to keep up this ridiculous charade?"

Tennant paced over to a tall mirror, took himself in, then headed back to the desk in the middle of the room. "I am a warrior!" he cried, gesturing dramatically with me as a prop. "A warrior trapped in this hideous charade. Can you imagine, little birdie, how it pains me to be nice and kind and polite, morning, noon, and night! How I yearn to lash out! To strike! To kill all the fools that surround me! But I cannot. No! That would not be in character for William Roger Tennant, great advocate of human virtues. Caretaker of all life-forms. Bah!"

<This guy's a psycho,> Rachel said, perched on the top of the open door. <I mean, even for a Yeerk, this guy's a psycho. We're talking, "Where's my medication? Lock me up in a rubber room" psycho.>

<Yeah,> I agreed weakly. <Nice psycho. Good psycho.>

Then, amazingly, Tennant turned his palm up and opened his hand. I struggled to my feet.

"There, there, little birdie." He stroked the feathers on my chest. "Good little birdie. Goooood leeetle birdieee."

He held me up right in front of his face. I resisted the temptation to take a chunk out of his nose.

"I have an idea, little birdie. If you can tell me your name, I will give you a treat. What is your name, little birdie?" he said. "Tell William Roger Tennant your name."

CHAPTER 10

"What is your name, birdie?" he repeated.

<Uh, do I have to answer this question?> I said to Rachel.

<Bail,> she replied. <Let's just get out of here.>

Tennant continued to stare straight into my eyes, that weird, "I'm about two Cokes short of a six-pack" smile still plastered to his face.

<I don't think he's going to let me go without an answer,> I said.

Noise in the hall! The thundering of padded feet. Hooves. Could Tennant hear them? He wasn't reacting.

<Guys! What's going on? Should we come in?> Jake said.

<No. Stay in the hallway,> Rachel said. <We're about to make a quick exit. You can take down Tennant when he follows. >

"Don't you know your name, little birdie?" Tennant hissed, eyes narrowing. "All my precious little birdies know their names."

<Make your move, Marco!> Rachel said.

I bent my legs, ready to spring.

Sudden suspicion darkened his face. "Unless you aren't one of my precious birdies at all."

I jumped backward, out of his hand. Flapped frantically, trying to get out of his reach.

"Unless you're one of the Andalite bandits in morph! Computer! Alert Status One! Andalite intruders!"

Tennant took a wild swipe at me. Missed. I shot toward the ceiling. Turned to follow Rachel to the doorway. Only ten feet away!

WHAM!!

<Aaaargh!> I hit the carpet beak first.

<Marco!> Rachel screamed.

One of my wings was broken, bent completely backward. I could feel one of the long wing bones popping through the skin.

"Fool of an Andalite," Tennant gloated. He kicked the huge dictionary aside and scooped me up in his sweaty palms. "Taking on such a weak morph! I admire your courage, but I'm afraid I will have to kill you just the same!"

56

<Aaaaaaaaaaaaahhhhhhh!>

Rachel dove for Tennant's head. Feetfirst, she dug her claws into his hair.

"What the . . . ?" Tennant growled.

<What the . . . ?> Rachel shot upward, away from Tennant's swinging hand.

Still holding his hair.

William Roger Tennant dropped me.

I hit the floor. The pain! My body was crushed. Every breath was pure agony. Vaguely I was aware of Rachel fluttering just over Tennant's head, his ponytailed toupee in her talons.

"Give me that!" Tennant screamed.

<Marco!> Jake shouted. <Are you okay?>

<I'm roadkill in here.>

<Rachel, lead Tennant into the hall!> Jake shouted. <Marco, demorph! Do you hear me? Demorph!>

Rachel flew into the hallway with Tennant's toupee. He chased after her.

<Hork-Bajir!>

<I count six,> Ax yelled.

<Ax, you and me on the Hork-Bajir,> Jake snapped. <Cassie, try to cover Marco. Rachel, get out of sight, demorph, remorph, and kick some butt. Tobias, we need you down here!>

I heard the sounds of battle in the long hallway. Tearing. Growling. Slashing.

I tried to concentrate. All I had to do was

morph out, and my injuries would disappear. But I was fading fast. I barely had the strength to think, let alone will myself to demorph.

<Watch out! Tennant's got a gun!>

<Spread out!>

"I'll kill all of you!"

BLAM!

A gunshot!

I felt the changes begin. My broken wings began to grow. Feathers turned to flesh. My body mass became larger, heavier.

My injuries slowly disappeared. My arms stretched out in front of me, miraculously healed. My ribs and torso returned to their normal size and shape. My lungs, able to breathe again!

TSEEEWWW!

Dracon beam!

I was nearly finished. The pain was gone. I could see straight. Think straight. Now what? Remorph? Firepower. My gorilla morph would do just fine.

I rolled under the huge desk and focused. My arms started to grow. Thick. Strong. Powerful enough to flip a car without breaking a sweat.

There was some heavy action going on in the hallway. The floor was pounding. The walls shaking.

"Kill them!" William Roger Tennant screamed. "Kill the Andalite bandits!"

Another shot!

I saw a Hork-Bajir stagger into the room. He slammed into the window, grabbed, slipped, and fell, wrapped up in translucent off-white window blinds.

The morph continued. Hurry! My friends needed me! Come on, Marco! Morph! Morph!

Wait! Something was wrong! My arms kept growing, but the rest of my body was shrinking! Getting smaller, smaller. I was barely a foot long! A foot-long torso with three-foot arms!

My skin began to feel dry, flaky. Scales? My head started sinking into my shoulders, flattening itself out into an arrowhead shape. An eye on each side of my face. My bottom lip extruded outward like I was trapped in kissing mode. Then my shoulders receded into the rest of my body until I was just a long, flat body with insanely huge arms.

I felt two slits opening, one on either side of my face. And suddenly, I couldn't breathe. Gills! I'd grown gills!

I was half-gorilla, half-trout!

<Noooooooo!>

<Haaaaaghhh!>

CHAPTER 11

The fish brain went berserk. I flopped around wildly on the floor.

<Marco. What exactly are you doing?>

Tobias?

I focused my distorted fish eye on the nearest window.

<I don't know, dude!> I yelled, feeling fairly well terrified.

<Well, demorph!> Tobias cried. <Get out of that morph! That's not right.>

Panic! I couldn't breathe! And my tiny body didn't store much oxygen. I was dizzy . . .

<Come on, Marco, you can do it. Focus!>

I whimpered. But the changes had begun. My

body started to grow. My arms to shrink. The slits in my cheeks disappeared. I gasped for air. Sweet, beautiful air.

<Cassie, behind you!> Jake yelled from the hallway.

William Roger Tennant screamed, "Kill them! Destroy them. I don't care if you burn this house down doing it!"

TSEEEWWW!

More Dracon beams!

<Rachel! Tobias! We need some help in here!>

TSEEEWWW!

<There's too many of them. Back up into the office!> Jake cried. <MOVE!>

TSEEEWWW!

<Marco,> Tobias shouted. <They're coming back this way, crank it up.>

I'd almost finished demorphing. I was human. With normal, functional arms and legs and lungs.

This wasn't necessarily a good thing. If Tennant saw me, identified me as Marco the kid — not the Andalite bandit — my life was over. My dad's life, too, for that matter.

In fact, all of my friends — everyone I knew — would be killed or taken prisoner by the Yeerks.

But if I didn't act now my friends might be dead anyway. I had to think of something!

The door to the hallway swung into the office. I hid behind it. It was a big door. Solid oak, about two inches thick.

TSEEEWWW!

<Keep moving!> Jake ordered.

I heard the panting of large mammals. The stomping of Hork-Bajir warriors.

Through the open door! Jake, Rachel, Cassie, Ax!

"Get them!" William Roger Tennant screamed. "They'll be trapped in the office! They'll be —"

WHAM!

I slammed the door. It hit something. Judging from the unrepeatable words Tennant shouted, it was his face.

<Marco! What are you doing out of morph?> Jake shouted.

"No time!" I said, locking the door. "We need to bail."

And we'd have to go through the window.

"Fools!" Tennant screamed from behind the door. "Break this door down! Disintegrate it!"

I looked around the room. What to use?

Webster's College Edition? The New York Public Library Desk Reference? The Collected Works of Leo Tolstoy? The chair?

No. William Roger Tennant's laptop. I

snatched it with both hands and yanked it off the desk, pulling out the cord in the process.

"Here's hoping he didn't back up his hard drive," I said, turning my back to the window. I spun the laptop around like I was doing the hammer toss. At the top of my arc, I let go.

The computer sailed through the air.

CRASH!

The massive window shattered into thousands of pieces of glass.

<Let's move!>

Tiger! Grizzly! Wolf! Andalite! All soared through the broken window. Scrambled to their feet. Ran off, over the wall of the compound. Safe.

BOOM! BOOM!

A battering ram! The office door buckled.

<Jump, Marco!> Cassie shouted back.

I dashed across the room. The office was on the first floor of the mansion. But the land sloped severely down toward the ocean.

There was at least a twenty-foot drop to the ground.

The tree. Its branches extended to within a few feet of the window. Below, a solid cement patio.

But what were my choices? Broken ankle — or life as a Controller.

I gritted my teeth, stepped up on the sill, and threw myself out the window. Kicked, flailed, snagged a branch with one hand.

Dropped out of the tree. Sprinted for a row of bushes that lined the wall surrounding the grounds. Dove behind it and curled myself up into the tiniest ball I could make.

Had William Roger Tennant seen me?

CHAPTER 12

"Why didn't you tell us about this problem?" Jake asked. We were gathered in Cassie's barn. This time I couldn't fake it. Couldn't pretend the morphing disaster hadn't happened. Tobias had seen the whole thing from outside the window.

"I don't know," I said. "I didn't think it was a big deal."

"No, you're right. You end up half-trout, half-gorilla while we're all playing pin the tail on the Hork-Bajir, why would that be a problem?" Rachel said.

"Everything turned out okay, didn't it?!" I snapped. "Besides, Rachel. You weren't exactly up front with us when you had that allergy to the crocodile morph. In fact, if I remember correctly, you lied to us about it. Said you were all better when you weren't."

Rachel winced, cocked her head, and said, "Maybe I'll just let someone else yell at you."

Jake turned to Ax. "Any idea why this is happening?"

<I am not sure, Prince Jake,> Ax replied. <We know that the morphing process requires focus and concentration. I have heard of cases in which emotional distress has negatively affected morphing ability.>

"Maybe the problem you're having with your dad is bothering you more than you think," Cassie suggested.

I gave Cassie a dirty look.

"I'm sorry, Marco," she said. "But if it's affecting your ability to fight, it's everyone's business."

"What problem with your dad?" Jake demanded.

"He's dating, all right?"

"That's *it*? We already know that. So is that the reason you're morphing into surf and turf?"

"Um, Jake," Cassie intervened. "His mom, may not be exactly dead? His dad, may not be exactly a widower?"

"Oh." Jake looked chagrined. "Sorry. It didn't click right away. Why didn't you say something before, Marco? I'm your best friend."

66

I shrugged. "Because it's no big thing." I laughed. A fake laugh. "I figure Ms. Rottenette will go away, eventually. How long can she possibly stand me?"

<I am confused,> Ax said. <Are you saying that your father is considering taking this woman as a new mate?>

"You could put it that way," Cassie said.

"But I'd rather you didn't," I added. "He's just —"

<Ah. Perhaps your father is Young and Restless. Those who are Young and Restless frequently change mates.>

"Okay, first thing, we smash Ax's TV," I said.

"Look, the problem here is Marco's ability to morph." Jake turned to me. "We can't have you going on missions in this state. For your sake and for ours."

"Really, it's not a problem," I protested. "I've just had a lousy couple of weeks, that's all. I'll get over it. Trust me on this."

"Maybe you need to talk to somebody," Cassie suggested. "Like a professional."

"Yeah, Cassie. 'Uh, Doctor Freud? My dad's thinking about remarrying. See, he thinks my mom is dead, but she's not. She's actually a slave to an alien race trying to conquer the planet. And did I mention the fact that I'm fighting this alien invasion myself? That I do it by turning into animals? Say what? What size strait-jacket do I wear?'"

"Well, okay," Cassie replied gently. "But what about us? We are your friends, Marco. You can talk to us. Keeping stuff all locked inside is what makes you get so stressed."

"Cassie, everyone here has problems. Ax is the only member of his species within a trillion miles who's not a Controller; you're a pacifist who spends half her time battling aliens; Jake is just a dumb jock trying to play General Eisenhower; Rachel is about three millimeters away from morphing permanently into the Terminator; and, oh, by the way, Tobias is a bird who lives in a tree and eats mice for breakfast. We all have problems. We are not exactly the poster children for Mental Health week."

"Dumb jock? Excuse me?"

"The point is we're all hanging on by our fingernails. What right do I have to go nuts?"

Cassie shrugged. "As much right as anyone."

"Yeah, well, that's not much, okay? We have things to do. I just need to get a grip is all."

Jake sighed. "Okay, let's focus here. Not to belittle Marco's problem, but we do have a mission. Taking down William Roger Tennant."

"Fat chance," Rachel muttered. "His public persona is solid gold. Except for the fact that he's a complete Looney Tune, his only flaw seems to be wearing a toupee."

Jake waved his hand in front of his face as if he were erasing a blackboard. "All right. It's obvious we're not going to figure out a solution tonight. We might as well go home and catch up on our homework. And Marco?"

"Yeah," I muttered. "I know. No morphing."

CHAPTER 13

The long walk home gave me a lot of time to think.

It took me only about two blocks to come to a conclusion.

I hated my life.

I'm not much for self-pity. It never does you any good. But there are times when it's pointless to deny that life sucks.

For a long time I had held on to the hope that my mother might come home again. Safe and sound. That my mom and dad and I might eat dinner together every night and go on vacation to the Grand Canyon and play Monopoly on rainy Sunday afternoons.

It was a long shot, my mom's coming home. I

knew that. A very, very long shot. It was a long shot even believing she might be alive. But still I'd had hope.

Then Ms. Rottenette had come along. Destroying the last of that hope. Decimating it.

I was going insane. Hard to believe that after all the craziness I'd been through since this war started, a simple, everyday, domestic problem would be the thing to push me over the edge.

Oh, yeah. And then there was the fact that we had no clue how to stop William Roger Tennant from recruiting for The Sharing on prime-time network TV.

And even if we did, I probably wouldn't be allowed to fight with the others. Because of my PROBLEM.

Bad day? Sure. But it was still early. Something could still screw up even worse. If I was really, really lucky.

What was I going to do for the rest of the night?

Homework? Not after a near-death experience. No, a near-death experience called for a couple of hours of vegging with my PlayStation.

My street. My house. I turned to walk up the driveway.

And stopped. Something was wrong. I looked quickly up and down the street. Nobody.

Looked back to my house. No lights. But the

garage was open and my dad's car was parked inside. And whose car was parked in the driveway?

I took a few steps. Slowly. *This would be a perfect end to my day,* I thought. A Yeerk ambush. Visser Three waiting for me in my own living room.

Had the Yeerks seen me at William Roger Tennant's house? Had they already identified me?

I crept around the back of the house. No lights on there, either. Slowly I walked back around front. Peeked through the large bay window into the living room. Too dark. I couldn't see a thing.

What should I do? Try a morph? I wasn't sure I could pull one off. And even if I could, one gorilla wouldn't be enough to stop Visser Three and a force of Hork-Bajir.

For a second I thought that maybe I was being paranoid. That my dad was already asleep. That he'd just forgotten to close the garage door. But that didn't explain the other car.

I thought about running off to find Jake and the others. Realized that by the time I got back with reinforcements, my dad could be dead. Or worse.

No choice. I reached for the doorknob. Turned it.

Slowly I opened the door.

"RrrrrrrRrrrrrrrrRrrrrrrRrrrrrrrrrrrRRRRrrrrrr."

Two clawed feet slammed into my stomach.

"Aaaaah!" I screamed.

"What the —?" a voice cried.

I swung my arms wildly, pushing the beast away.

"Arrarrarrarrarrarrarr!"

It attacked again. Shielding myself from its paws, I flipped the wall switch. The lights popped on.

"Get away from me!" I yelled.

"Arrarrarrarrarrarrarr!"

"Marco?"

It was my dad. He was sitting on the couch. Ms. Robbinette was sitting on the couch, too. They were sitting very close. In fact, Ms. Robbinette was more sitting on my dad than on the couch.

My dad jumped to his feet. His face was almost as red as the lipstick smeared across it.

"Euclid!" Ms. Robbinette shouted. "Stop! Sit! Be quiet!"

The idiot dog kept barking. And jumping on me. Only a foot and a half long, but it could jump three feet in the air. It would have been so easy to punt him across the room. Right through the kitchen window at the back of the house.

"What are you doing home?" my dad asked sheepishly.

"Uh, I live here?" I answered, pushing the dog away.

"Euclid! Stop!" Ms. Robbinette shouted again. "Honestly, I don't understand what's wrong with him."

I was tempted to give my opinion. Instead, I caught the mutt in midair. He tried to squirm away, but I squeezed him to my body the way a running back carries a football. I began to acquire him and he went limp.

"Ohh," Ms. Robbinette said, charmed by the sight of Euclid half-asleep in my arms. "See? He likes you, Marco."

I suppose you could call Ms. Robbinette pretty. She has dark hair and very smooth fair skin. I didn't care.

"We didn't expect you home so soon," my dad muttered while he tried to figure out what to do with his hands.

"Sorry."

"Usually you're out so late. You know. With Jake."

Euclid woke from his trance. He started to squirm and I dropped him. Immediately he clamped his jaws on the ankle of my jeans and started to pull.

"Euclid!" Ms. Robbinette yelled. "You know, Marco, Euclid does sense stress. Are you feeling stressed?"

I looked at my dad.

"Uh, aren't we all?" he said with an awkward laugh.

"I think I'll just go up to my room now," I said. I grabbed my PlayStation from under the coffee table.

"Nice seeing you, Marco," Ms. Robbinette said politely.

"Uh-huh," I grunted. My dad gave me a pained look.

I clumped up the stairs, Euclid attached to my ankle.

When I reached my bedroom door, I gently unhooked Euclid's jaws from my jeans, pushed him away, and slammed my door shut.

"Arrarrarrarrarrarrarrarrarr!"

I don't know how long he stayed out there barking. I hooked up my headphones to the TV and turned the volume up enough to drown him out.

CHAPTER 14

Normally I would complain. Normally I would point out that the very idea of this mission was insane. A ten on the Ten Point Insanity Scale.

But I couldn't. Couldn't say a word, because Jake had let me come along on the mission to infiltrate the Solid Citizen Awards and destroy William Roger Tennant's image.

We'd had to wait until Saturday evening for this mission. I'd spent a good part of the week practicing morphing in my bathroom. Gorilla. Osprey. Seagull. Wolf. Even creepy morphs like fly and cockroach.

Nothing. No problems. Every morph under control. Every morph whole and complete.

I seemed to have my morphing under control. I demonstrated a few morphs to everyone to prove this.

Finally, Jake decided to give me a chance. Besides, he needed me.

Big favor.

Our mission was simple. We'd seen for ourselves that Tennant's Yeerk was not a shining example of mental stability. I mean, in the dictionary next to "wacko" they could have used his picture. What we needed was to show that to the world. If we could get him to go off, in public, well, bye-bye guru.

The banquet was taking place at a big hotel near the beach, not far from William Roger Tennant's mansion. We'd been on a mission there before, when we tried to stop the Yeerks from infesting several of the world's most powerful leaders.

Security wasn't anywhere near as tight as it had been when presidents and prime ministers were guests. In fact, it was pretty easy getting in.

We morphed seagulls. Flew to the hotel. Found an empty room with a balcony. Landed on the balcony, demorphed, and walked inside. You'd be surprised how many people leave their balcony doors unlocked. I guess they don't think anyone is going to climb twelve floors up.

Then we took a service staircase downstairs,

found a bathroom near the restaurant kitchen, and morphed cockroach. Fortunately, we knew this place pretty well. Knew our way around. Which was a good thing since what a cockroach can see isn't worth seeing.

<There's too much foot traffic for us to crawl on the floors. We'd get squashed,> Cassie said.

<What's the alternative?> Tobias asked.

<The ceiling.>

<Say what?>

And that's when the mission became really interesting. Way too interesting.

<Okay,> Jake said, <this is easy: The big rectangle of light is the door of the bathroom. We'll see it, more or less, whenever someone opens the door. We head for that. Then across the hall, left, pass two doors, take the third door, and we're in the kitchen.>

<On the ceiling.>

<Yep. On the ceiling.>

<I see. And this is what you call "easy.">

<I remind everyone that we have been in morph for thirty of your minutes,> Ax said. <Dinner is scheduled to be served in twenty-five more of your minutes.>

<Ax?>

<Yes, Marco.>

<They're everyone's minutes, Ax. They're not *our* minutes. They're just minutes. Just minutes.

Okay? We're on Earth, *you're* on Earth, they are *everyone's* minutes.>

<Now we have been in morph for thirty-one of your minutes.>

<Okay, let's get this over with,> Rachel said. She was not showing her usual enthusiasm. Nothing scares me more than Rachel being scared.

We ran to the wall. Then we ran up the wall.

Here's what it's like being a roach. Imagine a car. Imagine one of those cool Jaguar convertibles. I mean, it's free in your imagination, right? Might as well have a cool car.

Imagine a red Jaguar convertible. Imagine yourself strapped to the underside, facedown, your nose about a millimeter from the road, and the idiot driving is going a hundred miles an hour.

A roach running across your floor looks pretty fast. But from down there, from the perspective of the roach, it's like someone strapped a thousand bottle rockets to your butt and fired them all at once.

I blazed across that dirty tile floor. And then screeched to a halt as my clever little roach antennae informed me that the world was going vertical. I crawled my two front feet up onto the wall, then my middle two, then my hind two feet, and up I went. Straight up. Straight up like someone had suspended the law of gravity.

Zooom!

Up the wall, tiny little claws snagging tiny little bumps in the paint. Up and up, wandering a little left, scaring myself by running into Ax, then straight back up.

I was a little brown robot. Up. Up. And then, a wall. Only it wasn't a wall, it was the ceiling.

<Are we sure we can do this?> Jake asked.

<Let me try,> some moron said. Wait, it was me! I had to. I was the weak link. I was the dubious morpher. I had to be cool.

I did as I'd done in going from floor to wall. Front two legs. Middle legs. Back legs.

<I'm on the ceiling,> I reported.

<Any problem?>

<Nope. No — aaaaaaaahhhhhhhhhhhh!>

Falling!

Falling!

Falling forever and ever, twisting and turning and . . .

Tunk!

I hit the floor. I'd fallen a hundred times my own standing height. Like a human falling off the Empire State Building. I'd landed on my back.

I was fine.

I motored back to the wall, back up the wall, and rejoined the others.

<I'm thinking we hug the angle between the wall and the ceiling,> I said.

<I was sure roaches could do ceilings,> Cassie said. <Sorry. Are you hurt?>

<Hurt? No. Interested in trying that again? No.>

<Let's go,> Jake said. <We have some food to infest.>

<Jake, have I mentioned how grateful I am to you for letting me come along on this little picnic?>

<Okay, let's get to the kitchen, find Tennant's food, and see if we can't get Mr. Mellow to freak out,> Jake said.

Around the bathroom. To the doorway. Down, onto the top of the door, then up to the hallway ceiling. Along the angle to the end of the hallway, then back to find the kitchen door.

At last we were there. We were in the kitchen. Mission almost accomplished.

And then Cassie said, <Jake? Something just occurred to me. This is a banquet, right? Hundreds of people. So how do we find which salad or whatever is Tennant's?>

There followed a long period of silence.

And then, still being an idiot, I said, <I have an idea.>

CHAPTER 15

I was not the ideal choice for the task, what with my recent morphing problem. But only Cassie, Ax, and I had the morph needed, and Ax couldn't be trusted in a kitchen in human morph. Far too much tempting salt and grease. And we needed Cassie with Jake and Rachel. So I got the job.

While the rest of the group stayed hidden under a large, unidentified appliance, I scurried to the employee locker room that adjoined the kitchen.

And how did I find the employee locker room, you ask? Smell, of course. There are no aromas quite so distinctive as human sweat and urine.

I found an empty toilet stall and demorphed.

"Another superhero adventure," I muttered to myself. "Does Batman go from bathroom to bathroom? No. Does the Silver Surfer surf the toilet stalls? No, he does not."

The locker room was empty. I dug through the lockers until I found a shirt and a pair of pants that didn't dwarf me. A bow tie that hooked together.

"Does Daredevil wear other people's dirty clothes? No. Spawn, maybe. Next time there's a superhero sign-up sheet I —"

I fell silent. A youngish man stepped into the room, ignored me completely, and quickly lit up a cigarette. I stepped past him, eyes down.

Noise. Lots of noise. Yelling, banging pots, roaring automatic dishwashers, knives chop-chop-chopping.

The kitchen was a swirling mass of activity. Half of the gymnasium-sized area consisted of several huge stoves, ovens, and slicing tables. Dozens of cooks were trimming steaks, slicing onions, mixing sauces.

Along one of the walls was the dishwashing area. On each side of it was a set of swinging double doors. These led to the banquet room.

The wall that separated the locker rooms from the kitchen was lined with several computer registers, an industrial-size coffeemaker, an espresso machine, and several large refrigerators. Jake and the others were most likely underneath one of the refrigerators.

Separating the cooks' area from the rest of the kitchen was a long row of stainless-steel shelves, stacked with plates. A bunch of guys were standing behind these shelves, mixing lettuce in huge bowls.

Waiters and waitresses scurried around. Stopped at the computers to punch in orders. Carried trays of drinks through the swinging doors, out to the banquet room.

Nobody noticed when I dropped to my knees in front of the refrigerator closest to the door.

"Guys?" I whispered.

<Marco? Is that you?> Jake said.

"It ain't Spider-Man." I laid my hand out on the floor. Five tiny cockroaches tickled their way onto my fingers, up my hand, and underneath my shirtsleeve.

I knew they weren't actual roaches. I knew they were my friends. I knew I'd been a cockroach myself. Didn't matter. They still gave me the creeps.

<Did you find the salads?> Jake asked.

"Uh-huh. I'm about to have a special one set aside for Tennant." I approached the salad station.

"Hey, dude, are you the salad guy?"

"The *what*?" he replied.

"The salad guy," I said. "The guy who makes salads?"

"You mean the *garde-manger*?" he hissed.

"Yes, that's exactly what I meant," I said. "Look, William Roger Tennant said he doesn't like tomatoes on his salad."

"Who's William Roger Tennant?" he sneered.

"Duh," I replied. He wanted snooty, he'd get snooty. "He's only the guest of honor at this banquet. He's the man. Well, him and Hanson. They're here, too."

"What is a Hanson?"

"Some blond kids who look like girls, who, for some reason, girls think are cuter than me," I said.

<Hey, Bob Dylan is cuter than you,> Rachel said from inside my sleeve. <Beethoven is cuter than you and he's been dead for a couple centuries.>

"How about if I crush you between my fingers?" I said.

"What?!" the cook snapped.

"Not you. Some bug. A bug with no taste, but that's not what matters. Tennant doesn't like tomatoes. Could you set aside a salad without tomatoes for him?"

"Whatever."

85

I watched as the guy reluctantly removed one of the salads from the shelves and picked the slices of tomato out of it.

"Here," I said, grabbing the bowl from him. "I'll take it." Holding it in my right hand, I lowered it out of his sight.

<Troops deploying,> Jake said.

When everybody was aboard, I turned to the salad guy again.

"I'm going to leave this salad on the top shelf here, okay? That way it won't get mixed up with the others. Don't forget to tell the waiter this special salad is for William Roger Tennant, okay?"

"Go away, little person. I am busy."

I set the bowl on the top shelf.

Now I had to join the party. No problemo. Morph to wolf spider, run out to a spot directly above the salad, drop into said salad, bide my time and scare the pee out of Tennant. Roaches and a spider? No one can see all that in his salad and not become slightly disturbed.

<Twenty of your minutes until we are served,> Ax said.

I hustled back to the locker room. After returning the clothes I'd borrowed, I found a dark corner in which to morph.

As soon as I'd finished, I came scurrying back out. I was feeling strange, like maybe I was still not done morphing, but that was only jitters. I ran for the wall and started to climb.

With my furry black paws.

My what?

"Oh my God!" someone screamed. "What is that thing?"

CHAPTER 16

No! Not again!

"It's like . . . oh, oh! It's like a miniature eight-legged skunk!" someone screamed.

"It's a mutant freak!"

"Kill it!"

"You kill it! I'm not going anywhere near that thing!"

I bolted underneath one of the refrigerators, my eight tiny paws scrabbling on the tile floor. Two sets of gigantic feet rushed toward me. I backed up against the wall.

Half-spider, half-skunk. Eight legs, all of them tiny skunk legs, with skunk paws and skunk claws. A third the size of a regular skunk, maybe four or five inches long. The wolf spider's pincerlike mouth. The skunk's long, white-striped tail.

And I still wasn't done changing. Eyes were popping in and out on my face. Open, closed, open, closed. Then, finally, I was looking at the world through a grand total of ten eyes: the spider's already bizarre combo of compound and simple eyes, plus two fully functional skunk eyes.

A lot of eyes. A lot of very twisted views of my environment.

<Marco. How's it going?> Jake said.

<Fine. Fine, everything fine,> I cried. A third pair of feet arrived. And the person attached to them had a broom.

<Did something go wrong with your morph?>

<No. Noooooo. No problem. Nope. But you know what? This is really not a good time to talk.> The third guy dropped to his knees and shoved the broom at me. It whacked me right in the face, crushing the spider's tiny mouthparts.

<Aaaaaahh!>

I bolted to my left. The broom followed.

"I got him!" Mr. Broom said. "He's coming out."

I ran out from under the refrigerator — right into a pair of waiting feet.

"Man, what the heck is that thing?"

"Oh, save us, it's the apocalypse upon us! The end of the world!"

89

"Don't let it get away!"

One of the feet swept across the floor and kicked me. I sailed against the wall. Being so small and light, the impact didn't hurt. Much.

Mr. Broom moved in. He flipped me away from the wall, toward the center of the room. I turned and scurried back into the locker room, six giant feet right behind me.

"Squash it! Squash it!"

A massive foot shot straight down at me! I dodged to the left. Another foot! I dodged to the right.

<Marco?> Cassie this time. <Are you okay?>

<Look, some people saw me, okay, I'm running, okay, I'm fine,> I lied, continuing my wild, zigzag pattern.

<Do you need help?> Jake demanded.

<Nope. All better now.>

I shot past a row of lockers. The showers were just ahead. A dead end. There was no way to escape.

Wait! I was half-skunk, wasn't I? I could try spraying. But could I do it before my pursuers crushed me?

I pulled a U-turn and sprinted for the toilet stalls. Again with the bathroom!

"Now we've got him!" Mr. Broom opened the stall door.

I raised my tail. Spray! Spray! Spray! I commanded the skunk.

Nothing happened! Nothing!

They surrounded me, cutting off any chance of escape.

"It doesn't stink like a skunk," the first pursuer said.

"Well, it ain't a skunk, you moron," Mr. Broom said. "It's too small. And look at all those legs."

"It's an omen, I tell you. It's a sign!"

"Yeah, but it's got a tail like a skunk."

"Whatever it is, squash it!"

Mr. Broom raised his bristled weapon. I cowered helplessly.

"Kinda feel sorry for it," the first guy said.

"What? I've never seen anything so ugly in my life!"

<Have you tried looking in the mirror?> I growled. I used private thought-speak. Jake and the others wouldn't hear.

The three of them froze. "Who said that?" Mr. Broom demanded.

<I did. Down here. Me. The creature you're trying to kill.>

"No way. I didn't know you were a ventriloquist, Charlie."

"I'm not."

"Maybe it is a sign."

<That's right, he's not a ventriloquist,> I said. <I am a talking half-skunk, half-spider. A skider. Or possibly a spunk.>

"Okay, this is too weird," the first guy said.

<Not as weird as it's going to get if you don't just drop the broom, turn around, and walk away.>

"What?"

<You heard me. Do it. Now.>

Charlie the Broom Guy was not impressed. "Or what?" he challenged.

<Or I'm going to turn into a ten-foot monster and pop your heads off like dandelions.>

"Oh, yeah. Right."

<All right, gentlemen. But don't say I didn't warn you.>

It was risky. Stupid even. But what else could I do?

I began to demorph. And grew. Fast. From six inches long to a foot to two feet to four —

"Aaaaaaaaaaaa!" Broom screamed.

His friends agreed.

"Let's get out of here!"

They ran out of the locker room.

Yes! I finished demorphing and snuck up to the doorway of the kitchen to see what was going on.

"I'm telling you, Marcel," Broom whined. "There's a monster in there! We all saw it!"

"It talked to us in our heads!"

"We live in the final days! Fire and brimstone will rain down upon us!"

A booming voice cut them off. "Idiots! Ah hev a room full of guests out zere! Do yew sink I am heving time for your *stupide* games?"

"But —"

"Look," Marcel continued, "I dun't care what yew are doing wis your free tem, but when yew are here, I expect yew to be working! *Comprenez?* Now get beck to work!"

<Marco?> Jake. <Can you hear me?>

I couldn't answer, of course. Instead, I put on the old busboy clothes again. No more morphing for Marco today.

<The salads are supposed to be served in ten of our minutes,> Jake went on. <I mean, ten minutes. Are you in place?>

I finished dressing and went back into the kitchen. I walked up to the salad station.

"I'm gonna make sure you guys reach your destination," I mumbled. Tennant's special salad was now surrounded by at least two dozen other salads. It would be easy for a careless waiter to give Tennant the wrong one.

"What?" My pal the *garde-manger* had heard me.

"Nothing."

He made a brushing-away gesture with his hands. "Shoo."

93

"YEW! What are yew doing stending around?"

Marcel. I recognized the voice.

"Get to work!"

"But —"

"No buts! Yew need somesing to do? Empty ze peeg bucket!"

"Ze what?"

"Yew are mucking me? Go! Take care of it! *Immédiatement!*"

The guy marched off.

"What's a pig bucket?" I said.

The *garde-manger* grinned. "It's that thing by the dishwasher."

That thing was a huge plastic garbage can — overflowing with uneaten food.

"Shovel's out back," the *garde-manger* said. "Go. Or I'll call Marcel back."

CHAPTER 17

I haven't decided what I'm going to do when or if I survive this war and actually become an adult. But one thing I know for sure. It won't involve working in a restaurant.

As an Animorph, I've done lots of disgusting things. Heck, I've been lots of disgusting things. But I can tell you, nothing I've done before quite compared to emptying that pig bucket.

It only took a few minutes. But they were the grossest few minutes of my life. Shovels full of chicken bones, half-eaten hamburgers, slime-covered macaroni. All mushed together to make a cold stew more aromatic than a fly's wildest imaginings.

95

Oh yes. The life of a superhero is a glamorous one.

When I was finished, I raced back into the kitchen from the garbage alley. Waiters and waitresses surrounded the salad station. I squeezed through the throng, looking for the roach-infested, tomato-less salad.

Gone! It was gone!

"Hey," I cried to the salad guy. "What happened to William Roger Tennant's salad?"

He shrugged. "Gone."

"Did you tell the waiter the salad was for Tennant?"

"He can take the tomatoes off if he doesn't like them."

"Aaahhh!"

<Marco?> Jake called out from far away. <Is that you carrying us now?>

I squirmed through the crowd and bolted for the banquet room. Burst through the swinging door. Searched the banquet room for William Roger Tennant.

About twenty round tables covered with white cloths were arranged around the room. And at those tables sat people in tuxedos and fancy dresses and an unusually large number of over-dressed girls my own age or younger.

Those would be the Hanson fans.

Against the wall, to the left of the swinging

kitchen doors, was a long rectangular table, raised a few feet off the floor and covered with a long white tablecloth. The dais. Where the guests of honor sat. In the middle of the dais was the podium, from where William Roger Tennant would make his acceptance speech.

<Okay, Marco,> Jake said. <We're being set down now. We'll just have to hope we're where we need to be.>

I sprinted up the few steps of the raised platform. Three guests sat on each side of the podium. William Roger Tennant was seated to the immediate left of the podium. The podium blocked my view of his salad.

The three Hanson kids were to the right of the podium. I sidled up behind them, grinning and trying to look like I was supposed to be there.

<Marco,> Jake called out. <We're moving out.>

I reached Tennant just in time to see him lean over to the person on his left and say, "These tomatoes look delicious!"

"Aaaaahhhhhhhhh!"

The scream came from behind me.

<Uh, that doesn't sound like Tennant,> Tobias said.

<It sounds like Zac!> Cassie cried.

I spun around. Zac Hanson had fallen backward in his chair. His two brothers leaped to his aid.

"Aaaaahhhhhhhhh!" Zac screamed, frantically brushing at the cockroaches in his lap.

"Aaaaahhhhhhhhh!" a girl in the audience screamed back.

"Aaaaahhhhhhhhh!" Zac yelled.

"Aaaaahhhhhhhhh!" cried a woman in a long red dress.

"Aaaaahhhhhhhhh!" Within seconds, the room was filled with the sounds of women screaming, chairs overturning, and men yelling "Sssshhhh!"

<Run! Outta here!> Jake yelled. Five cockroaches sprang from Zac Hanson's pants and fluttered toward the ground.

<Watch out for the feet!> Cassie cried.

"Aaaaahhhhhhhhh!" women and girls screamed.

<That horrible noise!> Ax cried. <Even with this insect's poor hearing I feel as if my head is going to explode!>

<It sounds just like a Hanson concert,> Tobias said.

A cockroach scurried by my foot. I snatched it.

<I have been captured!> Ax cried.

"It's me, man. I've got you," I whispered.

Four roaches shot out of sight beneath the long tablecloth.

<Who's here?> Jake asked. Rachel, Tobias, and Cassie all answered.

<Marco has me,> Ax said, crawling up my wrist.

<Ooookay,> Jake replied. <That could have gone better. Guess it's time for Plan B.>

<Someday when this is all over people will ask us about the war against the Yeerks,> Tobias said. <Let's leave this part out.>

CHAPTER 18

Plan B made Plan A look brilliant by comparison.

Ax morphed to human and dressed in a second dirty uniform. Once I convinced him an apron was not a cape we did okay. I needed Ax. I had a feeling no one was going to let me get near the dais. I was associated with the regrettable roach incident.

I remained human, in my own busboy outfit. No problem. Ax and I could work together. As long as I was there to keep an eye on him. See, Andalites don't have mouths. No sense of taste. And when Ax morphs to human, and suddenly has a mouth full of taste buds, he can be dangerous.

We emerged into the banquet room.

Hanson was nowhere to be found.

William Roger Tennant was still sitting at his end of the dais, chatting with the man to his left.

And that's when Marcel appeared behind me. "Yew are needed in ze beck. Ze peeg bucket, she is full again."

The guy was grinding my final nerve. But if I started complaining it might occur to Marcel that I was not one of his many anonymous busboys after all.

"Ah weel dew ze peeg bucket," I said. I could just dump it in the alley and rush right back. Still no problem. I ran for it.

<Marco? Ax?> It was Jake. <Are you guys in place?>

<I am here, Prince Jake,> Ax replied.

<Where is Marco?>

<He ees cleaning up ze peeg bucket.>

Long pause. I heard all this in my head as I dragged the stupid trash can of glop into the alley.

<Okay, whatever. We've found a way to demorph and remorph as fleas,> Jake said. <We're at the far end of the table, left of the podium. Who's going to deliver us to the target?>

<Whoever it is, hurry. I'm surrounded by bare ankles, here, and I'm hungry,> Rachel said.

<Marco is not here.>

101

<Okay, I guess it has to be you, Ax,> Jake said.

"No!" I yelled in frustration at a skanky alley cat.

<I am quite capable of this simple maneuver,> Ax said snippily. <Marco was merely concerned that I would go postal. But I have no mail.>

<Is anyone else getting that sinking feeling?> Tobias muttered.

I slammed the trash can against the wall and turned to run back inside. Yanked the handle. It didn't move. I was locked in the alley!

<Okay, Ax,> Jake said. <We're clinging to the underside of the tablecloth. Lift up the edge, farthest corner, and you'll see us. At least I think that's where we are. Aiming a flea anywhere is about as accurate as firing a Nerf gun blind.>

BamBamBam! "Hey! Open the door! I'm trapped out here!"

<Yes, Prince Jake. I am moving toward you. I smell delicious grease.>

"Uh-oh. LET ME IN!"

Nothing! Had to get back inside. Around the front. No other way. I ran down the alley.

<I see you, Prince Jake. My hand is quite near to you.>

<Okay, everyone, smell the blood and jump.>

Down the alley. Jump over the cat. Slip. Up, run!

<You are safely on my hand now,> Ax reported.

<Okay, now you just have to get us to the target: Tennant's head.>

<I believe I can do so by performing as the other workers are performing.>

<Performing?> Cassie asked.

<They are removing the plates from the seated humans.>

Around the corner. Front door of the hotel just ahead. I was panting.

<Okay, that's good,> Jake said. <Just clean off the plates, Ax.>

"No, you idiot, don't tell him that! Don't say 'clean off'!" I cried at the uniformed doorman.

Past the baffled doorman. Through the red-carpeted lobby.

<The humans are refusing to cooperate,> Ax reported. <I am merely attempting to clean off their plates, and yet they are behaving in a hostile, aggressive manner.>

<What?!> Jake snapped.

Wham! Through the banquet room doors, lungs gasping for breath. I leaped on an empty chair, trying to see over everyone's head.

There, on the dais, about three people down from Tennant, was Ax. His face was covered in smeared, orange Thousand Island dressing. Pieces of lettuce clung to his chin and decorated the front of his busboy jacket.

As I watched in helpless horror he reached for another plate.

I ran. Like what's his name in *The Bodyguard*. Like Clint Eastwood in that movie about the Secret Service. I ran, pushed, shoved.

Ax yanked the plate from a woman's hands. It came away suddenly. Leftover salad flew. Flew straight into William Roger Tennant.

Tennant yelped.

Ax licked the plate, his tongue extended to full maximum. Then he moved methodically on. He reached for Tennant's plate.

<Soon it will be time to jump on the target,> Ax reported blandly, as if everything was otherwise perfectly normal.

<We're ready.>

Tennant was standing up, menacing, upset, but controlling it. I was just a few feet away, bounding along the dais.

Ax grabbed Tennant's plate. Tennant held on.

"I'm not quite done yet, young man," he said.

"You must give me the plate." Ax yanked the plate and at the same time reached up with his flea-loaded hand and shoved Tennant down into his seat.

<Jump!> Ax said.

<Everyone go!> Jake ordered.

I was close enough to hear Tennant growl, "I am gonna kick your —"

I grabbed Ax with both arms. Held him back and yelled, "Sir, we're not really busboys, we're just really big fans, could we have an autograph?"

CHAPTER 19

We got the autograph. Amazing what people will put up with if you flatter them. Then we did our best to melt into the crowd. It would have been easier except Marcel was prowling, looking for us.

We yanked off our uniforms. I looked around frantically. Empty chair! Just one, but it would do.

"May we join you?"

It was a table full of old people in suits or dresses, depending. One of them may have been our mayor. I'm not sure.

"There's only one chair."

"It's okay, we're very good friends." I sat down and yanked Ax down onto my lap.

"Ladies and gentlemen, our guest of honor, host of *Contact Point,* and author of several best-selling books — William Roger Tennant!"

The crowd rose to its feet and applauded enthusiastically. The emcee stepped aside and Tennant approached the podium.

"Thank you," he said, smiling hypnotically and raising his arms as if to embrace the entire audience. "Thank you so much."

<We're in position,> Jake said. <We are under the toupee. Biting has begun.>

"Such wonderful people you are," William Roger Tennant sighed when the applause finally died down. "I am truly honored to receive the Solid Citizen Award. You know, people often ask me how I've managed to be so successful in my field," Tennant began. "I give them a one-word answer."

<This is so gross,> Cassie complained.

"And that one word is —"

He stopped in mid-sentence. His eyes twitched. His lips twisted into a frown.

"— love," he gasped finally.

"Tell them it's working," I whispered.

<Marco believes it is working,> Ax translated into thought-speak.

<We are,> Tobias replied. <We're biting.>

"It takes a great deal of love to excel in any field," William Roger Tennant continued through gritted teeth. His eyes bulged. A large vein popped out on his temple. Sweat trickled down his cheeks. "You have to love what you do, and love the people you do it for."

<What's he doing?> Jake asked.

"He's twitching," I whispered.

<He is showing discomfort,> Ax answered.

<That's good,> Cassie said.

<But he seems to be maintaining his composure.>

<Geez,> Tobias groaned.

"Love is the core principle of my philosophy," Tennant said loudly. He paused and took a deep breath. Scratched the top of his head with his pinky, ever so gently. The tension in his face started to fade. His eyes stopped twitching. His brow relaxed.

"It has been my mission to share my philosophy with the world. And the responses of people like you here in this room have shown me that my message has some merit."

"They must be stopping," I said. "Tell them to keep it up!"

The mayor's wife gave me a long, hard look. I smiled back.

<Do not stop,> Ax said. <He seems to be regaining control.>

<We're biting as hard as we can,> Rachel replied testily. <I've got what feels like a five-

foot-long spike dug into this guy's scalp, all right?>

<This is the grossest thing we have ever done,> Cassie complained.

"If you really believe in something," Tennant continued, showing less and less strain with each word, "you must be willing to sacrifice all, to endure anything, to fight against all adversaries, no matter how large or small. You must be willing to never give in, never surrender, until the battle is won. The battle, ladies and gentlemen, the battle . . . to love! Ladies and gentlemen, thank you again for this honor. Good night."

The room exploded with applause. Flashbulbs popped. The crowd rose to its feet.

Tennant rushed off the dais. Made his way through the adoring crowd, smiling and waving.

"Thank you, William Roger Tennant!"

"We love you, William Roger Tennant!"

Ax looked at me. "This was not a successful mission."

"No. It really wasn't. Now get up off my lap."

Not successful was the understatement of the year. And the others didn't even realize just how badly it had gone. No one but me knew about the twisted morph.

We headed for the exit. I couldn't get out of this place fast enough.

<What is it with this guy?> Rachel muttered

from her perch on Tennant's head. <Is he made of Teflon?>

<As crazy as this plan was,> Jake said, <it should have worked. On any normal human, it would have worked. I am seriously out of ideas.>

<There's got to be a way,> Rachel said. <There must be something irritating enough to make Tennant go off in public.>

Irritating?

No. It wouldn't work.

Or would it?

CHAPTER 20

My dad was not home when I got there. I was relieved. I didn't even care if he was out with old lady Robbinette. I was in a seriously bad mood.

Bad enough the whole fiasco of trying to freak Tennant. Worse that I still didn't have my morphing under control. Which meant I didn't have my mind under control.

I watched some TV. I went online, got into a chat about music, and ended up calling everyone morons. I was shaking when I finally hit the "sign-off" button.

Cookies. I needed some cookies.

I went to the kitchen. I found a half-finished package of Pepperidge Farms. I poured some milk.

"You know what?" I told the milk carton. "I don't care if William Roger Tennant signs people up for The Sharing. If they're that dumb, forget 'em. Why am I going to get myself killed for them?"

The milk carton had no immediate response. Maybe it wanted to think that over.

I went to the living room, lay on the couch, and turned the TV back on.

The doorbell rang.

"Oh, man, don't be someone selling newspapers or whatever," I muttered as I went to the door and opened it.

"Cassie?"

"Hi. Can I come in?" She didn't wait for me to answer but just sort of pushed her way past me.

I followed her back to the living room. She turned off the TV and looked expectantly at me.

"What?"

"You could offer me a cookie."

I handed her the bag.

"You have something to tell me?"

"No."

"So why are you here?"

"I'm here to listen to you."

I laughed. "What, are you a shrink now?"

She shrugged. "You said it yourself: We can't exactly go to see counselors, can we?"

112

"Look, I'm fine."

"No, you're not," she said. "Jake bought it, Rachel bought it, but I didn't. Something went wrong. I heard it in your thought-speak. You blew another morph."

I sat down. I was sure I'd covered. I was sure. But of course this was Cassie. Cassie who knows what people are feeling about five minutes before they do.

"Did you tell Jake?"

"No. And I won't."

"Why not? What happened to it being everyone's concern?"

"Because I want you to know you can trust me. You know, enough to talk to."

I realized I was bouncing my leg nervously. I stopped it. "Look, it's nice of you and all, but —"

"I know all the buts: We're all under pressure, we're all barely hanging on, and besides, you're a guy, and the 'guy code' is that you never talk about your feelings."

I snagged the cookies back from her. She took my milk. "Who told you about the 'guy code'? That's top secret."

"Marco, I have both my parents at home with me. They don't know anything about Yeerks or about us, but I have them, and I know they love me, and they're there when I get home. Jake's the same. Rachel's parents are divorced but —"

"— And look what a pillar of mental health she is," I said with a laugh.

"Rachel has her mom, and she talks constantly to her dad, and she has her little sisters, and she has me. But Marco, for two years after your mom died, or at least everyone thought she was dead, your dad totally fell apart. You were the man of the house. No one was there to take care of you."

"I take care of myself."

Cassie sat beside me. She put her hand on my arm.

"Cassie, does Jake know you're flirting with me?"

She ignored my weak attempt at a joke. "And then we found out your mom was still alive. Only she wasn't your mom anymore. Her body had been taken over by a Yeerk. And she was the enemy. Marco, in the space of a few awful months you've gone from believing your mother is dead to almost literally having to try and destroy her."

"And you think maybe that's stressful?" I deadpanned.

"I think it would have crushed most people," she said. "That mission against her and Visser Three, you were setting her up to take a fall. You were intimately involved with leading Visser One, your mother, into a trap that —"

"Shut up! Shut up!"

I jerked up off the couch. I had my hands over my ears. Stupid. I took my hands down. They were trembling. "Look, Cassie . . ." I started to say with exaggerated calm. But then I forgot what I wanted to say.

I could see her. On that mountaintop. Her sudden realization that it was me who had brought her there. Marco. Me. Her son. Her host's son. Not some ruthless Andalite warrior but her own son . . . Visser Three's troops and ships closing in. The cliff giving way.

Falling.

And later, Rachel had come to me and said that her body could not be found. That maybe she was still alive.

And Rachel had understood that she wasn't doing me any favors because it was so much better to know, to know for sure anything, even to know something terrible as long as the torture of uncertainty was over. . . .

"What did I do?" I whispered.

"You're in a war, Marco. You're here, in your own living room, eating cookies and watching TV and going to school on Monday, but you're in a war. Bad things have happened to you."

"Tobias isn't losing it. Ax isn't losing it. Look at them, they're both all alone. My God, Tobias isn't even human anymore."

115

"Marco, you don't know what they've gone through. They'd never tell you."

"Guy code," I said.

"It doesn't matter what they feel anyway, you know? You have to deal with what you feel."

"I feel like you drank my milk."

Cassie hung her head. She looked beat. Probably was. I was. I felt bad, like I'd let her down. She'd come over, as tired as she was, to try and help.

"I feel better," I said.

Cassie rolled her eyes. "Look, Marco, don't talk to me if you don't want to. Don't even talk to Jake even though he is your best friend. If you have to keep everything inside, I guess that's how you are. But you need to at least be honest with yourself."

"Okay," I said noncommittally. "I'll do that."

She got up, sighed, and headed for the door. Then she stopped. "You know, at the clinic we're always getting animals who are hurt or injured by humans. By jerks who shoot at them for no reason, or try and burn them, or whatever. And I used to get so mad. I just hated those people. And I'd feel like I was wasting my time because, you know, there's always some jerk with a twenty-two. I'd rage about it. But my dad told me, 'Deal with what *is*.'"

I was confused. "What's that mean?"

116

"It means, the animal is hurt. Help the animal." She came back over to me and took my hand. "Or in your case, Marco, it means that the Yeerks are here, your mother is Visser One, and your dad is lonely. None of that *should* be. But it *is*."

CHAPTER 21

<Ready, Marco?> Tobias asked.

<Am I ready? Was Sitting Bull ready for General Custer? Was General Schwarzkopf ready for Saddam Hussein? Was General Washington ready for whoever's butt he kicked?>

<So, you're saying you're ready then?>

<Oh, yeah. I'm ready.>

Every muscle in my body was alive, electric, eager to run, to jump, to attack! I had long claws and sharp teeth, specially designed to tear my prey apart. Limb from limb. I had a motor that could run nonstop for hours. Without even a thought of tiring!

<All right, he's just reaching the gate.>

Not that I needed to be told this. My superkeen ears could hear him just fine, even over the roar of the surf. My nose, thousands of times more sensitive than any human's, had caught wind of him the moment he walked out his front door.

I heard the familiar sound of the key turning in the lock, the squeal of the hinges as the door swung open. My nose was bombarded with his scent, so strong, so familiar. Only this time there was a new smell added to the usual mix of soap, deodorant, and laundry detergent.

Fear.

A smell even more powerful than Right Guard or Old Spice. It was a smell I loved. A smell I lived for. A smell that attracted me like a shark to blood.

The growl began in the back of my throat, an unconscious, instinctive warning to my prey that said: "I'm coming to get you."

<Stay back,> Tobias said. <He hasn't come out yet. He's looking for you.>

Stifling the powerful urge to attack, I stayed crouched in the bushes just outside the gate.

<Okayyyy,> Tobias said tentatively, <he's coming — NOW!>

SLAM! The gate shut behind him. William Roger Tennant took off down the beach, jogging at twice his usual speed. Pretty fast.

But nowhere near fast enough. I shot out of the bushes. I was on him in seconds.

I had powerful legs made for running and jumping. I had claws and teeth that could tear a man apart. But these were nothing compared to my most horrifying weapon of all.

My voice.

"Ararararararararararararrrrrrrrrrr!" I barked.

He increased his speed. But he knew he was doomed. The smell of his fear, even stronger now, guided me like a heat-seeking missile.

I pounced. Three feet off the ground! I bit into his shirt with my iron jaw and held on, making a swimming motion with my feet so my claws could scratch his bare legs and arms.

"Stupid —!" Tennant screamed. Along with a few other words I can't repeat.

He was ten times my size. A six-foot-tall human against a foot-and-a-half-long toy poodle. One well-placed kick or punch and he could have crushed my ribs or skull.

But he couldn't do this. See, there were too many witnesses. Way too many people on the beach who would be horrified to see the great animal lover William Roger Tennant beating a poor, innocent poodle to death.

A couple of dudes playing Frisbee stopped to watch the action. Broke out laughing when they realized what they were seeing. A six-foot-tall man being tormented by a crazed toy poodle.

Tennant stopped dead in his tracks. The sudden stop was enough to cause me to lose my grip and send me flying. I landed on my feet and spun back around to face him.

"I will kill you, Andalite," Tennant hissed, low enough for no one else to hear.

Dogs don't have very good vision. It's a little fuzzier than human sight. And while they can sort of see colors, what they see is not much more colorful than the picture on a black-and-white TV.

But I could read the expression on William Roger Tennant's face well enough. His mouth was bent in a vicious frown. His eyes were seething with hate. His right cheek twitched uncontrollably.

"Do you hear me, you cursed beast?" he hissed. "I will kill you!"

I pounced again. Got a grip on his shorts that nearly tore them off his hips.

You know the little girl in the Coppertone ad? With the doggie pulling off her swimsuit? Tennant looked just like that little girl as he dashed back toward his mansion, desperately holding up his shorts with one hand.

I let go when we reached the gate. He quickly

unlocked it and stepped inside. Not before giving me one last leer before shutting it behind him.

<Good job,> Tobias said, landing on a tree just above me. He turned his head and looked down at me with one seagull eye. <This plan just might work.>

CHAPTER 22

For the next two days, Tobias and I followed William Roger Tennant like paparazzi on an actress. Hoping to go for an unmolested run on Wednesday, he took his limo out to a park near the river. We followed, and I was there to catch him before he'd jogged his first mile.

Thursday afternoon, Tennant was scheduled to give a speech at the convention center downtown. I was waiting for him just outside the main doors. Before he had a chance to climb the stairs I'd ripped a sleeve off his suit jacket and torn a huge hole in the seat of his pants.

He cancelled the speech.

Thursday night after the show, Tennant met up with some local sponsors for a late dinner. In red-tailed hawk and owl morph. Tobias and I followed the limo to the restaurant. I morphed again, and the minute his foot hit the pavement, I was peeing on it. His sponsors watched in horror as I pounced on him, grabbed hold of his tie with my teeth, and almost pulled him down face-first onto the sidewalk.

Of course, he couldn't fight back. Couldn't kick me. Couldn't slap me. Not with so many fans and sponsors and non-Controllers watching. All he could do was smile.

My dog senses could tell he wanted to kick and slap me. Could tell by the way his pulse went through the roof when he caught sight of me. By the way his breathing became short, clipped, and tense. The way his teeth ground together like a bowl full of marbles.

Mostly I could tell by his smell. It wasn't a smell a human could detect. Too subtle. But this aroma, a combination of fear and total hatred, was a magnet to my nostrils. It fed me. It inspired me. Like a shot of adrenaline, it helped me jump high enough to reach his tie. Bite hard enough to rip even through his leather jeans. Run fast enough to catch him, no matter how much of a head start he got.

And I loved every second of it.

Let's face it. Everything messed up about my life could be blamed on the Yeerks. My mom. My

124

dad's misery. Now the complication of his new girlfriend. For months, my friends and I have been living in fear, our lives changed forever by this invasion. Facing ridiculous odds. The threat of death or capture always there, twenty-four hours a day, seven days a week.

We'd experienced things no person should ever have to experience: war and devastation, betrayal and defeat. And all the skin-crawly horrors of morphing.

Win or lose, I'll have nightmares for the rest of my life.

Now, unexpectedly, it was payback time. Not some morally troublesome action that might result in a serious injury or even death, some violence that would eat away at me. This was clean. This was pure. I had a Yeerk in my poodle sights. And he was going to suffer.

Was I taking a sadistic pleasure in it all? Yes. I was.

Friday evening. The big night. I headed home.

"Hey, you're just in time," my dad said when I walked into the kitchen. He flicked off the stove and shoveled the pieces of chicken he'd been frying onto our plates. He was jittery. Jumpy.

"Something wrong, Dad?" I asked him.

"No, no," he muttered nervously, avoiding eye contact. He sat down across the table from me. "What makes you say that?"

I watched as he lifted his fork and bobbled his knife, nearly managing to impale his own thumb.

"You, uh, thinking about switching to base nine for your math needs?"

He stared at his shaking hands and laughed. "Just call me poker face." His smiled faded. He put down his fork and knife and rubbed his hands with his napkin. "Uh, Marco, I was hoping we could talk."

"Together or separately?" I replied.

"Uh, together, I guess," he said, oblivious to my joke. "You see, well . . . oh, man, I've never been good with words. But, you know I loved your mom very much, Marco."

I felt my heart stop. Sucked in my next breath like it was coming through a straw.

He paused. He wanted me to say something. He wanted me to make this easier for him. I should have. But I didn't.

I heard Cassie in my head telling me to deal with what is. No. I didn't like the "is." The "is" was about to get worse.

"Losing her was so hard for the both of us. But she's been gone over two years now. And, and . . . and she's not coming back."

He wiped tears from his cheeks. I hated him right then. How dare he cry? Who was he to cry? He was betraying her. He was setting her aside, consigning her to the past. He was killing her, that's what he was doing.

"I — we — can't spend the rest of our lives grieving for her. And, for the first time since she died, I've actually been happy. Nora and I —" He paused. "I think it's what your mom would have wanted. She would have wanted us to move on with our lives. To be happy. Doesn't that make sense?"

No. No, because she was my mom. She was his wife. So no, Dad, no, cut out the weepy crap, cut out the self-pity, no! She's my mom!

I didn't say anything. What could I say? I knew I was wrong, knew I was being unfair, and I didn't care. But I couldn't say anything.

"Nora and I have been talking about getting married, Marco. But we won't do it without your okay."

"Yeah? And what if it's not okay?" I said. I could hardly hear my own voice.

He sighed. His eyes turned vacant, distant. The way they'd looked for a large part of the past two years. I hadn't missed that look. I hadn't missed it at all.

"Marco, we're a team, you and I. We've been through a lot together. If you say no, I'll accept that."

Fine. So it was on me. Great. Typical. Yeah, why not? I'll decide if my dad is happy or not, if my mom is still my mom. I'll decide if she lives or if she dies so that I, the Great Marco, the great cold-blooded Marco can prove how tough I am by leading her into a trap, setting her up . . .

I felt pain. I was digging my fingernails into the side of my head.

I was going to explode. Some artery in my head was going to blow apart. It was too much. Way too much.

"I'm out of here," I said.

I got up and ran for the door.

CHAPTER 23

We met on the roof of the TV studio. It was windy. Not easy to land with that much of a breeze.

We demorphed from our various bird morphs. Tobias stayed as a hawk.

"Okay," Jake said. "Here's the plan. Ax and I hit the control booth. Marco gets harassment duty, as usual. We may only have a few seconds, maybe a minute of airtime before we get shut down. We have to catch, *on camera,* William Roger Tennant losing control. Rachel and Cassie will be in the studio as backup. Tobias is outside, on lookout. And keeping an eye on the crew's preshow meeting. Got it?"

Everyone looked at me. Waiting for my usual

129

lame joke about how we were heading toward certain doom. I let them wait.

"Something wrong, Marco?" Rachel said.

"What could possibly be wrong?" I replied finally.

Cassie gave me a long, hard look. She wasn't going to say anything, but she was making sure I knew that she knew I was messed up.

We morphed flies. Entered the building through a fresh air duct. It led us right into the studio. From there, we went to our separate posts.

The plan was simple. And only slightly more idiotic than the banquet fiasco. The network guy was in the studio to watch a live broadcast of Tennant's show. And we were in the studio to make Tennant look like the lunatic he was.

That's where I came in. I was supposed to morph to Euclid and bait Tennant — before the show began. Had to be before the show began: Tennant was just controlled enough not to blow it in public. We had learned that at the banquet. He was crazy, but he was crazy in private.

I would go after him. Alone on the set. Right where he could finally get his hands on me. When he attacked me — which he would — Ax would have cut into the computers and would send out a live feed across the country.

A great idea. For everybody but the bait: me.

Tennant would try and kill me. His chances of accomplishing that goal before Cassie or Rachel could stop him were pretty good.

If Cassie and Rachel weren't shot first by a Controller on the crew.

If it worked we'd all have a big laugh. If it didn't . . .

So far, everything was going according to plan. William Roger Tennant was sitting on the set in his comfy chair. Arms and legs crossed. Eyes closed.

Tobias and Ax had scouted the place earlier in the week. They'd made a crude sketch of the layout. We'd memorized it.

And they'd made notes about Tennant's usual behavior. Like the fact that every night before the show Tennant chilled for about twenty minutes. Alone with only his Lava lamps for company.

I wondered what the thing was with the stupid Lava lamps. Did they remind him of the Yeerk pool? Or did he just miss the sixties?

The director, the cameramen, and the rest of the crew were at their usual preshow meeting. This time with Mr. UPN.

<You know, it's really a shame I can't get to meet that UPN guy,> I said. <I have a great idea for a new *Star Trek* series. See, it's way in the future and the Federation has been broken up by the Dominion and only three ships are still —>

<Marco?>

<Yeah, Jake.>

<Don't talk to the UPN guy. Poodles do not pitch show ideas.>

<Tell me about it later,> Tobias said. <Sounds cool. I always thought the whole Federation thing was just too easy and —>

<Puh-leeze!> Rachel exploded. <Next mission: girls only.>

Tobias was keeping watch on the meeting through the conference room window. Though we knew at least some of the crew and probably the director were Yeerks, we were pretty sure Mr. UPN was not.

The studio itself was low budget. Not much larger than a three-car garage. Pre-air time, the place was eerily dark. The bubbling Lava lamps gave the air a weird reddish glow. Tennant's chair was in one corner of the set. A pair of TV cameras faced the star's chair. In another corner a small control room had been built. One wall of the control room was a large window.

Opposite the control room and just out of camera range was another small area, separated from the studio by unplastered Sheetrock walls. Tennant's dressing room. In it was a desk with a lighted mirror and a barber's chair. Next to the desk was a fire exit door with an "alarm will sound" bar across it.

Cassie, Rachel, and I landed in the dressing room. I demorphed. Rachel and Cassie buzzed under the desk. They would morph wolf and get me out of there if Tennant went totally ballistic.

<Okay,> Jake called out to us in thought-speak. <We have the control room to ourselves. Ax has morphed to human. He's setting up for the broadcast. Everybody check in.>

<I've got the meeting,> Tobias said from outside. <The crew and the network people are drinking coffee and yapping. I'll let you know when they're coming.>

<Everything's fine here,> Rachel reported. <Just waiting. Wish I could morph grizzly or elephant or something with more firepower than a wolf. But I guess there's no room.>

I finished demorphing, then took a few breaths to get my strength back. I focused on Euclid.

Euclid. The most annoying dog the world had ever seen. I hated that dog. And now my dad wanted him to move in with us?

I mean, forget the misery of my mom's disappearance. Forget the fact that every day during fifth period I would have to do algebra for my stepmother. Having to live with that mangy mongrel would drive any kid insane.

I felt the changes begin.

My hands. Transforming themselves into

133

paws. Little white paws with long, dull claws. Long claws that clacked and scratched against the kitchen floor when the obnoxious mutt raced around the dinner table, yapping at the top of his lungs until someone finally dropped him some scraps.

My legs grew shorter, skinnier. My thick, human leg muscles began to shrink, tightening into taut, sinewy springs. Muscles powerful enough to propel the cursed beast three feet — four feet — in the air. High enough to jump on my lap and fatally ruin my concentration during key points of video games.

I felt fur growing along my back. Thick, curly white fur that made my nose itch. That stuck to my favorite black jeans.

The transformation was nearly complete. I was a five-foot-long poodle. With a human boy's head.

Not for long.

My head began to grow. Larger. Wider. My nose stretched out in front of me. My eyes grew dim, as if I'd just put on a pair of sunglasses. My ears shrank and slid up the side of my head.

My mouth, too big to be a poodle's mouth. Uh-oh. Long white muzzle, blunt, not delicate like the poodle's.

Uh-oh. Definite uh-oh.

<Marco, your morph is going weird!> Cassie yelled.

What was happening? What was I?

I held up one paw to look at it. Moved and slammed against a wall. I was hot, I knew that much. My fur was a mix of kinky and straight. The straight fur was more clear, more transparent than truly white.

Polar bear? I was half-poodle, half-polar bear?

I was a poo-bear?

<Aaahhhh!>

And then, the instincts kicked in. The polar bear's cold-blooded predatory intensity joined to the Daffy-Duck-on-espresso lunacy of the poodle.

I could smell prey. I saw a pair of wolves, eyes glittering. Not prey. Predators. Nope, I wasn't going after them. I wanted something more like a seal. Yeah. Or else a mouse.

Then, I heard the sounds. Movement. Something living. Just on the other side of the wall.

I rose on my hind legs. Then, I dropped down again and charged.

<Marco,> Rachel cried. <What are you doing?>

WHAM! Eight hundred pounds of hyperactive poodle smashed through the Sheetrock wall. Prey! Possibly a seal!

135

Tennant jerked around.

"Aaahhhh!"

I crossed the fifteen feet between us in seconds. Tennant dove out of the way just before my hubcap-size front paws smashed his chair into pieces.

<Jake, Marco's lost it!> Cassie warned.

<What do you mean he's —> Jake demanded from the control room.

<She means he blew another morph, and now he's a poodle the size of a Volkswagen,> Rachel said.

My prey dashed. Ran for the door. Big mistake. Running just made me excited. Running was like an advertisement: Yes, I am the prey, please come and eat me.

Four massive steps and I was on him. I shoved him with my huge paws. He flew through the air and hit the wall.

The seal was cornered. Down.

Time for lunch.

CHAPTER 24

"Noooo!" Tennant wailed, cowering like a trapped rat. I felt no pity for him. I didn't know about pity. I was the poo-bear.

<Marco, get a grip!> Cassie screamed. <You're going to kill him.>

<Why not?> I said. <He's a Yeerk. He's a seal-Yeerk.>

Everything was black-and-white in this morph. Simple. Kill the prey. Kill the enemy. Nothing else mattered.

And yet, some small part of my mind said, <Seal-Yeerk? Poo-bear? Huh?>

Tennant curled into a little ball in the corner. He yelled, "Help me! Help me!"

But the crew didn't seem terribly interested in helping him. Mostly they were running.

<You're lost in the morph, Marco,> Cassie said calmly. <Get a handle on it. You had another mixed-morph. Now get control. *Get control.*>

<Everybody, stay where you are,> Jake said.

<Don't worry,> Rachel said. <I am not going anywhere near that thing. If I was in grizzly morph, sure, but . . .>

<I am ready for the broadcast, Prince Jake,> Ax said calmly, as though nothing unusual were happening.

<Come on, Marco,> Cassie encouraged. <It's going to be okay. Remember the mission?>

The mission?

I poked Tennant's huddled body with my paw. Watched him shrink and shudder.

<What's going on, Marco?> Cassie said soothingly. <Talk to me. We're your friends. Talk to us, talk to me and —>

<Talk my butt,> Jake snapped. <Marco. Cope. *Now.* That's an order.>

It was like a bucket of ice water dumped on my head.

It was like waking up from an intense dream. Fast. Painful. Slowly my mind grasped control.

<Jake, he's going through some bad stuff in his life,> Cassie said. <He's stressed. His dad is —>

<Cassie, you know I love you and admire you, but be quiet,> Jake said. <You listen to me, Marco. We have zero time for your self-pity. I don't care what your problems are. You deal with this, right now.>

I started to shrink.

My body deflated like a balloon with a pinhole.

My head, shrinking. Becoming a normal poodle head.

<That's not exactly enlightened behavior, Jake,> Cassie shot back, obviously angry. <If he's having stress —>

<Cassie, he's not you, he's not Rachel, he's not even me. He's Marco,> Jake said. <What he needs is to pull his head out of his rear end and remember what he always says.>

What I always say? What was he talking about?

Jake said, <Life is either tragedy or comedy. Usually it's your choice. You can whine or you can laugh.>

I laughed. Laughed in recognition. *Oh, yeah. I do say that.*

I was completely poodle.

"What the —?" Tennant said, scrambling to his feet.

<Good job, Marco,> Cassie said.

Or was it?

I sprinted away from Tennant.

"Andalite," Tennant hissed. He no longer carried the fear scent. He smelled of pure hatred. "You've made a terrible mistake. You should have killed me when you had the chance. I will not show you such mercy."

<Ready, Ax,> Jake said.

Tennant reached down and grasped an electrical cord that was lying on the floor. He yanked one end of it out of the wall, the other from the stage light it was attached to.

CRAAACK!

Tennant's makeshift whip could slice me in half.

<Oh, man,> I whimpered.

<Get back on stage, Marco,> Jake said. <We're ready to roll.>

<Just let them get the picture, Marco,> Rachel said. <Then we'll get you out of there.>

I cowered behind the remains of Tennant's chair.

CRAAACK!

He missed me by inches.

"This is going to be so therapeutic," Tennant cackled.

<Stay right where you are, Marco,> Jake said. <Draw him into camera range.>

<The meeting is over,> Tobias called. <They're leaving the office!>

CRAAACK!

The cord slapped across my back! Like being hit with a smoldering-hot stick!

"Yipe!" I cried pathetically.

<The crew and the network people are coming down the hallway,> Tobias said. <They'll be there in ten seconds.>

<Hang on, Marco,> Cassie said.

<Do I have a choice?>

<Ready, Ax?>

<Yes, Prince Jake.>

William Roger Tennant dropped the whip, reached down, and grabbed me by the neck. Lifted me in the air. Turned around to face the cameras. Wrapped his hand around my throat and held me up in front of his face.

He began to squeeze. I whined and struggled.

"Come now, Andalite," Tennant said, his eyes raving. "You aren't going to die on me that easily, are you?"

<And . . . we are live!> Ax announced. <Heeeeeere's Marco!>

Suddenly the entire stage was bathed in blinding light.

Choking! My head felt like it was going to explode. My blurry vision grew more hazy. My body was going limp.

I was too weak to struggle.

"Die, Andalite! Die!" Tennant screamed,

141

oblivious to the lights and the hum of the cameras.

"What the hell is going on here?" someone shouted. "My God, Tennant! What are you doing?"

"Get away from me!" he yelled. "I will kill you all!"

"What are these dogs doing here?"

"Andalites," a crew member hissed.

"Die, you filthy mutt, die!" Tennant screamed.

"What do you mean, we're on the air? Cut the feed, for crying out loud! Cut the feed!"

"I'll squeeze your guts out through your ears!"

"He's crazy!"

A mass of bodies surrounded me. Hands reached for Tennant. Subdued him. Pried his fingers from my throat. I dropped to the floor.

<Cassie! Rachel! That's enough, get Marco outta there!>

<We're already on it, fearless leader,> Rachel said.

"Grrrrrrrr . . ."

Rachel and Cassie growled. Snarled. Slunk toward the mass of men and women.

"Holy —" someone shouted. "Those aren't dogs. They're wolves, man! They're wolves!"

"What is going on here? What kind of production is this?" a man thundered.

142

The UPN guy?

"This is madness. You want to put this lunatic on the air? Try Fox, I'm not interested."

"It's not . . . it's . . . you don't . . ." Tennant stuttered. "It's all just a misunderstanding!"

I was gasping, forgotten on the floor. I wondered if this would be a bad time to mention my idea for a new *Star Trek*.

<Boys and girls,> Jake said, <I believe our work here is done.>

CHAPTER 25

"**I** am very pleased with the atmospheric conditions we are experiencing today. The lack of clouds have allowed the sun to show through, thus making electrical lighting unnecessary. Uh-NESS-a-sarry. Uh-NESS-ussery. Also, the lack of precipitation has kept my artificial skin from becoming uncomfortably damp, which —"

"Ax?" I interrupted.

"Yes, Marco?"

"Stop that. Please."

"Come on, Marco," Tobias said. "He's just practicing his small talk. We spent hours on it last night."

"Thank you again, Marco," Ax said, "for invit-

144

ing me to this primitive yet interesting cere-
mony."

"My pleasure, Ax-man. Do not go near the
buffet table."

"How do you define 'near'?"

"Ax, I'm telling you: No food."

"It really was a lovely wedding," Cassie said.

"Yeah," I agreed. "But I can't believe Rachel
cried."

"Hey," Rachel shot back. "Lots of people cry
at weddings."

"Yeah, I just didn't know you had actual tear
ducts, Rachel."

"There's a lot of things you don't know about
me, Marco," she replied. Her tone seemed almost nice.

Rachel? Nice? To me?

"It's the tux, isn't it?" I said. "That's why
you're being nice to me. The tux gives me a
whole new look. Very Sean Connery. Very Pierce
Brosnan."

"Don't," Tobias warned.

"I have no choice," I said. "I have to say it:
Bond. James Bond."

It was two weeks after our battle with William
Roger Tennant. They had been two very busy
weeks. And for once, the busyness had nothing
to do with Yeerks or alien battles of any kind.

Thanks to Ax, William Roger Tennant's freak-out was cut into a local TV broadcast. Naturally, the news networks ran with the video. CNN ran it roughly four thousand times.

No one had seen Tennant since.

After the William Roger Tennant incident, I spent a couple of days thinking about what my dad had said. About moving on with our lives. Making a new start. About our being a team.

I'd also thought about what Cassie had said, about having to deal with what "is," things as they are, and not how I wished they were.

And I remembered Jake's immortal words of comfort. "I don't care what your problems are. You deal with this, right now."

But mostly, I remembered what I've always believed. What my mom taught me. That while some things are just plain awful, most things in life can be seen either as tragic or comic. And it's your choice. Is life a big, long, tiresome slog from sadness to regret to guilt to resentment to self-pity? Or is life weird, outrageous, bizarre, ironic, and just stupid?

Gotta go with stupid.

It's not the easy way out. Self-pity is the easiest thing in the world. Finding the humor, the irony, the slight justification for a skewed, skeptical optimism, that's tough.

Anyway.

The past was over and done with. My mom, Visser One . . . I had to set that aside and think about my dad. And me.

Time to get on with my life.

Good-bye, dream. Hello, Euclid.

So, before the wedding I had a long talk with my dad. I told him the marriage was okay with me.

I was best man. You can fill in your own joke. Rachel filled in several.

The day after the wedding we started moving Nora in. She understood I wasn't going to call her "Mom." I have one mother. That's all I'll ever have. Whether she's alive, or not.

A few days later, it was all done. Nora was with us now. The dog, too. I didn't mind Nora. I could see where maybe we'd get along okay.

I still disliked that dog.

I was coming home from school when I heard the phone ring. It rings more often now with Nora around because she gets calls from parents asking why their kids are flunking math.

I decided not to answer. Let the machine get it.

And then, I heard her voice.

"Marco, if you're there, pick up."

My mother.

Don't miss

#36 The Mutation

"They're dead," I said unnecessarily.

"Are you sure?" Rachel said in an oddly small, thin voice.

<They'd have to be. How could they . . .> Tobias's logic trailed off.

<If you like, I will examine the bodies, Prince Jake.>

"Good idea," I said. "You do that, Ax."

"Ax is the man," Marco mumbled.

His hooves ka-klunking on the painted metal deck, tail blade angled forward, poised for attack, Ax stepped through the narrow doorway.

Cassie went with him. I guess this was a medical situation, to her.

Ax leaned one of the bodies forward gently, respectfully. Cassie looked at what he was showing her and gasped.

The two of them came back.

<They are dead humans,> Ax stated. <They

have been preserved. Stuffed with a substance I cannot identify without further, more detailed examination, and sewn up the back with a stringy vegetative material.>

"I am so out of here," Marco said. "Jake, we have to go. Now."

"Marco? Shut up." Rachel said, but more like she was trying to quiet her own fears.

"Mummies? Like, what? Like Egyptian mummies?" I asked, feeling stupid.

"Sewn up the back," Marco muttered. "Who cares what style? Dead is dead."

"The bodies are in remarkable condition," Cassie said, sounding like she was talking from some other place, not connected to her own body.

<I am unable to identify the culture or people responsible for this, Prince Jake. This is so irrational and strange that I assume it must involve humans.>

Two dozen Japanese pilots gazed sightlessly at a briefing map. Ready for the attack. Where? Pearl Harbor? Midway? Some forgotten battle?

They'd been the enemy then. Didn't look or feel like the enemy now.

"Let's get out of here. Back out on deck."

I felt marginally better outside.

SCREEEEECCCHHH!

Instinctively, I ducked.

A seagull! The bird swooped only inches above our heads and landed on the metal railing bordering the deck.

"Look at the eyes on that thing!"

The creature I thought was a seagull was not a normal seagull.

Its eyes were enormous. They covered the entire sides of its head and touched over its beak. And unlike a normal seagull's eyes, this bird's eyes were bright blue.

<Eyes adapted to a perpetually dim environment?>Tobias guessed.

As if in response the bird squawked, spread its wings, and took off.

"Are we certain the Sea Blade came through this Museum of Lunacy?" Marco said. "Cause I, for one, am all for bailing."

I frowned. "No, we're not sure. But we have to assume it did. And our mission's still the same."

"Destroy the Sea Blade before Visser Three finds the Pemalite ship," Rachel said.

"And avenge Hahn's death," Cassie added softly.

"Let's go airborne," I said. "It's probably safer and we can cover more ground. Tobias, stay hawk. Everyone else, go owl."

Owl. A morph I hoped would allow us to see more clearly in the dim light.

To explore silently.

To defend ourselves if we had to against mutant seagulls and whatever other odd creatures we might find.

Whatever other *live* odd creatures.

A few minutes and we were off again. We followed the river farther into this macabre underwater world.

Hundreds of ships for countless square miles!

German U-boats. A 1930s vintage tramp steamer. Pieces of junked motorboats. A Polynesian raft.

Rows of periscopes. Broken hulls. Propellers. Ships' wheels. Rudders and radar equipment. Deck furniture from luxury ocean liners.

And bodies.

Preserved pilots and passengers. Eighteenth-century European crew and twentieth-century tourists. Whalers. Fishermen.

<It looks like a collection,> Cassie said. <Almost orderly. Deliberate.>

<Yeah. Mr. Psycho's Nautical Toy Box and Graveyard,> Marco added grimly.

<Or a sicko director's movie set,> Rachel said. <Is anyone else expecting to run across, say, the *Titanic?*>

<These ships and boats are from everywhere,> Marco pointed out. <Atlantic, Pacific. Thousands of miles away. That galley has to be from the Mediterranean. This is impossible.>

With my keen owl's eyes I detected a slight glow a few hundred yards ahead. As we got closer to the light I saw that it was coming from the far end of a narrow tunnel.

A tunnel into which the nautical graveyard and the river were rapidly narrowing.

<What now, Jake?> Rachel asked.

I hesitated again. But only for a moment.

To go on was to lead my team — my friends — further into the unknown. And from what we'd just seen on the Japanese carrier, there was a good chance the unknown was seriously weird.

And probably very dangerous.

Or go back. Turn around.

Forget the search for the Sea Blade. Leave it to chance whether Visser Three ever found the Pemalite ship. Stole its secrets. Used those secrets to further the Yeerk invasion of Earth.

The visser. The Abomination responsible for the sickening recent torture and murders of Hahn and forty-nine other innocent Hork-Bajir.

<Keep going,> I said.

Twenty-five feet from the light. Fifteen. Ten.

<What the —!>

<Whoa!>

WHHHOOOSSSHHH!

Sucked through to the other side!